THE MASTER OF THE PRIORY

Annie Haynes was born in 1865, the daughter of an
ironmonger.

By the first decade of the twentieth century she lived in
London and moved in literary and early feminist circles.
Her first crime novel, *The Bungalow Mystery*, appeared in
1923, and another nine mysteries were published before her
untimely death in 1929.

Who Killed Charmian Karslake? appeared posthumously,
and a further partially-finished work, *The Crystal Beads
Murder*, was completed with the assistance of an unknown
fellow writer, and published in 1930.

Also by Annie Haynes

The Bungalow Mystery
The Abbey Court Murder
The Secret of Greylands
The Blue Diamond
The Witness on the Roof
The House in Charlton Crescent
The Crow's Inn Tragedy
The Man with the Dark Beard
The Crime at Tattenham Corner
Who Killed Charmian Karslake?
The Crystal Beads Murder

ANNIE HAYNES

THE MASTER OF THE PRIORY

With an introduction
by Curtis Evans

DEAN STREET PRESS

Published by Dean Street Press 2016

All Rights Reserved

First published in 1927 by The Bodley Head

Cover by DSP

Introduction © Curtis Evans 2016

ISBN 978 1 911095 29 3

www.deanstreetpress.co.uk

To

PAUL NICHOLS

VICAR OF

ST. MICHAEL'S, PADDINGTON

The Mystery of The Missing Author
Annie Haynes and Her Golden Age Detective Fiction

The psychological enigma of Agatha Christie's notorious 1926 vanishing has continued to intrigue Golden Age mystery fans to the present day. The Queen of Crime's eleven-day disappearing act is nothing, however, compared to the decades-long disappearance, in terms of public awareness, of between-the-wars mystery writer Annie Haynes (1865-1929), author of a series of detective novels published between 1923 and 1930 by Agatha Christie's original English publisher, The Bodley Head. Haynes's books went out of print in the early Thirties, not long after her death in 1929, and her reputation among classic detective fiction readers, high in her lifetime, did not so much decline as dematerialize. When, in 2013, I first wrote a piece about Annie Haynes' work, I knew of only two other living persons besides myself who had read any of her books. Happily, Dean Street Press once again has come to the rescue of classic mystery fans seeking genre gems from the Golden Age, and is republishing all Haynes' mystery novels. Now that her crime fiction is coming back into print, the question naturally arises: Who Was Annie Haynes? Solving the mystery of this forgotten author's lost life has taken leg work by literary sleuths on two continents (my thanks for their assistance to Carl Woodings and Peter Harris).

Until recent research uncovered new information about Annie Haynes, almost nothing about her was publicly known besides the fact of her authorship of twelve mysteries during the Golden Age of detective fiction. Now we know that she led an altogether intriguing life, too soon cut short by disability and death, which took her from the isolation of the rural English Midlands in the nineteenth century to the cultural high life of Edwardian London. Haynes was born in 1865 in the Leicestershire town of Ashby-de-la-Zouch, the first child of ironmonger Edwin Haynes and Jane (Henderson) Haynes, daughter of Montgomery Henderson, longtime superintendent of the gardens at nearby Coleorton Hall, seat of the Beaumont baronets. After her father left his family, young Annie resided with her grandparents at the gardener's cottage at Coleorton Hall, along with her mother and younger brother. Here Annie doubtlessly obtained an acquaintance with the ways of the country gentry that would serve her well in her career as a genre fiction writer.

We currently know nothing else of Annie Haynes' life in Leicestershire, where she still resided (with her mother) in 1901, but by 1908, when Haynes was in her early forties, she was living in London with Ada Heather-Bigg (1855-1944) at the Heather-Bigg family home, located halfway between Paddington Station and Hyde Park at 14 Radnor Place, London. One of three daughters of Henry Heather-Bigg, a noted pioneer in the development of orthopedics and artificial limbs, Ada Heather-Bigg was a prominent Victorian and Edwardian era feminist and social reformer. In the 1911 British census entry for 14 Radnor Place, Heather-Bigg, a "philanthropist and journalist," is listed as the head of the household and Annie Haynes, a "novelist," as a "visitor," but in fact Haynes would remain there with Ada Heather-Bigg until Haynes' death in 1929.

Haynes' relationship with Ada Heather-Bigg introduced the aspiring author to important social sets in England's great metropolis. Though not a novelist herself, Heather-Bigg was an important figure in the city's intellectual milieu, a well-connected feminist activist of great energy and passion who believed strongly in the idea of women attaining economic independence through remunerative employment. With Ada Heather-Bigg behind her, Annie Haynes's writing career had powerful backing indeed. Although in the 1911 census Heather-Bigg listed Haynes' occupation as "novelist," it appears that Haynes did not publish any novels in book form prior to 1923, the year that saw the appearance of *The Bungalow Mystery*, which Haynes dedicated to Heather-Bigg. However, Haynes was a prolific producer of newspaper serial novels during the second decade of the twentieth century, penning such works as *Lady Carew's Secret*, *Footprints of Fate*, *A Pawn of Chance*, *The Manor Tragedy* and many others.

Haynes' twelve Golden Age mystery novels, which appeared in a tremendous burst of creative endeavor between 1923 and 1930, like the author's serial novels retain, in stripped-down form, the emotionally heady air of the nineteenth-century triple-decker sensation novel, with genteel settings, shocking secrets, stormy passions and eternal love all at the fore, yet they also have the fleetness of Jazz Age detective fiction. Both in their social milieu and narrative pace Annie Haynes' detective novels bear considerable resemblance to contemporary works by Agatha Christie; and it is interesting to note in this regard that Annie Haynes and Agatha Christie were the only female mystery writers published by The Bodley Head, one of the more notable English mystery imprints in the early Golden Age. "A very remarkable feature of recent detective fiction," observed the *Illustrated London News* in 1923, "is the skill displayed by women in this branch of story-telling. Isabel Ostrander, Carolyn Wells, Annie Haynes and last, but very far from least, Agatha Christie, are contesting the laurels of Sherlock Holmes' creator with a great spirit, ingenuity and success." Since Ostrander and Wells were American authors, this left Annie Haynes, in the estimation of the *Illustrated London News*, as the main British female competitor to Agatha Christie. (Dorothy L. Sayers, who, like Haynes, published her debut mystery novel in 1923, goes unmentioned.) Similarly, in 1925 *The Sketch* wryly noted that "[t]ired men, trotting home at the end of an imperfect day, have been known to pop into the library and ask for an Annie Haynes. They have not made a mistake in the street number. It is not a cocktail they are asking for…"

Twenties critical opinion adjudged that Annie Haynes' criminous concoctions held appeal not only for puzzle fiends impressed with the "considerable craftsmanship" of their plots (quoting from the *Sunday Times* review of *The Bungalow Mystery*), but also for more general readers attracted to their purely literary qualities. "Not only a crime story of merit, but also a novel which will interest readers to whom mystery for its own sake has little appeal," avowed

The Nation of Haynes' *The Secret of Greylands*, while the *New Statesman* declared of *The Witness on the Roof* that "Miss Haynes has a sense of character; her people are vivid and not the usual puppets of detective fiction." Similarly, the *Bookman* deemed the characters in Haynes' *The Abbey Court Murder* "much truer to life than is the case in many sensational stories" and *The Spectator* concluded of *The Crime at Tattenham Corner*, "Excellent as a detective tale, the book also is a charming novel."

Sadly, Haynes' triumph as a detective novelist proved short lived. Around 1914, about the time of the outbreak of the Great War, Haynes had been stricken with debilitating rheumatoid arthritis that left her in constant pain and hastened her death from heart failure in 1929, when she was only 63. Haynes wrote several of her detective novels on fine days in Kensington Gardens, where she was wheeled from 14 Radnor Place in a bath chair, but in her last years she was able only to travel from her bedroom to her study. All of this was an especially hard blow for a woman who had once been intensely energetic and quite physically active.

In a foreword to *The Crystal Beads Murder*, the second of Haynes' two posthumously published mysteries, Ada Heather-Bigg noted that Haynes' difficult daily physical struggle "was materially lightened by the warmth of friendships" with other authors and by the "sympathetic and friendly relations between her and her publishers." In this latter instance Haynes' experience rather differed from that of her sister Bodleian, Agatha Christie, who left The Bodley Head on account of what she deemed an iniquitous contract that took unjust advantage of a naive young author. Christie moved, along with her landmark detective novel *The Murder of Roger Ackroyd* (1926), to Collins and never looked back, enjoying ever greater success with the passing years.

At the time Christie crossed over to Collins, Annie Haynes had only a few years of life left. After she died at 14 Radnor Place on 30 March 1929, it was reported in the press that "many people well-known in the literary world" attended the author's funeral at St.

Michaels and All Angels Church, Paddington, where her sermon was delivered by the eloquent vicar, Paul Nichols, brother of the writer Beverley Nichols and dedicatee of Haynes' mystery novel *The Master of the Priory*; yet by the time of her companion Ada Heather-Bigg's death in 1944, Haynes and her once highly-praised mysteries were forgotten. (Contrastingly, Ada Heather-Bigg's name survives today in the University College of London's Ada Heather-Bigg Prize in Economics.) Only three of Haynes' novels were ever published in the United States, and she passed away less than a year before the formation of the Detection Club, missing any chance of being invited to join this august body of distinguished British detective novelists. Fortunately, we have today entered, when it comes to classic mystery, a period of rediscovery and revival, giving a reading audience a chance once again, after over eighty years, to savor the detective fiction fare of Annie Haynes. *Bon appétit!*

Curtis Evans

THE MASTER OF
THE PRIORY

Chapter One

CARLYN HALL was a big, rambling house, having no architectural pretensions whatever. Nevertheless it was a roomy, comfortable abode with its wide passages and big, low roofed, raftered rooms. Originally it had been little more than a farm-house, but as the Carlyns grew in wealth and importance, and began to rank with the county, successive owners had enlarged and improved it according to their own ideas, each man throwing out a room there, a window here, as seemed good in his eyes. Time, the kindly, had thrown over the whole a veil of ampelopsis and ivy, had mellowed the old walls and sown them with lichen and stone crop.

It looked very pleasant and homelike to-day as the last rays of the setting sun fell across the many-gabled roof, touching it with molten gold.

Tea was being laid beneath the great beeches that had been in their prime when the Carlyns were only yeomen. Mrs. Carlyn, the mother of the young squire, sat in her accustomed place by the big wicker- table, and beside her Barbara Burford, the vicar's daughter, was playing with Bruno, Frank Carlyn's favourite setter.

Suddenly Bruno pricked up his ears, then shaking off Barbara's hand he sprang up and bounded round the side of the house.

The girl laughed. "No need to tell us that Frank has come home."

Mrs. Carlyn smiled in response. "No, Bruno is devoted to his master. I don't know why Frank did not take him to-day. He generally does. Barbara, there is one thing I must ask you. Is it true Esther Retford has left her home?"

"I believe so," Barbara answered with apparent unwillingness.

Mrs. Carlyn turned pale. "What will her poor father do? He worshipped her. Barbara, who is the man?"

The girl shook her head. "Nobody knows, some stranger probably."

Mrs. Carlyn sighed. "I hoped so. I did hear a whisper that— Ah, here is Frank!"

Barbara's long eyelashes flickered, the colour in her cheeks deepened as the young master of the house stepped out of his study window and crossed the lawn towards them.

At first sight his pleasant, boyish face looked unusually worried and preoccupied, there were two vertical lines between his level brows, and his mouth was firmly compressed. But, as he caught sight of the girl sitting beside his mother, his expression changed, his face lighted up in a way that made it look wonderfully bright and attractive.

"Why, Barbara," he exclaimed as they shook hands, "you are almost a stranger. I haven't seen you for ages. What have you been doing with yourself?"

"Oh, well"—Barbara laughed, yet with a touch of constraint in her manner that did not escape Mrs. Carlyn's watchful eyes— "I have been rather busy. And this is a good-bye visit too. I am going to stay with Aunt Freda to-morrow."

"Oh, really! I am sorry to hear that—sorry for our sakes, I mean," Carlyn said as he took his cup of tea from his mother's hand.

But his tone lacked warmth, and after a quick glance at him the girl turned back to Bruno, who had installed himself at her feet. She drew his long silky ears through her fingers and fed him with dainty pieces of bread and butter.

Mrs. Carlyn glanced at her son. "Where have you been, Frank? You look hot and tired."

"I have been dismissing Winter," he answered shortly. "The coverts are in a disgraceful state, and when I spoke to him about it he was so insolent that I dismissed him then and there."

There was a pause. Carlyn's eyes watched every movement of Barbara's fingers. The girl did not look up; the hand that was caressing Bruno stopped suddenly for a minute, then went on again mechanically. At last Mrs. Carlyn spoke:

"I am very glad to hear it. We shall be well rid of Winter."

"Yes," her son assented without any enthusiasm. He was not looking at Barbara now, his eyes had strayed to the Home Wood, in the midst of which stood the humble cottage of John Winter, his head gamekeeper.

"I shall not be sorry to make a change," he went on. "But I cannot help thinking of the man's wife. It will be jolly hard lines on her."

"Ah!" Mrs. Carlyn drew in her breath.

Barbara stood up suddenly. "I must be getting back. Father will be expecting—"

Mrs. Carlyn put out her hand. "Not yet, Barbara, dear. I want to consult you. I suppose Mrs. Winter will go with her husband, Frank. He is a young man and will presumably be able to support her in another situation."

"Oh, support," Carlyn echoed, with a shrug of his broad shoulders. "I wish I could get you to take an interest in her, mother. Or you, Barbara. It is obvious that she belongs to a class above Winter's. And the man is a brute. He ill-treats her; I am not sure he does not beat her." He clenched his right hand.

"Oh, I should hope not," Mrs. Carlyn said in her placid tones, though her eyes looked troubled. "Anyhow, it is an awkward thing to interfere between man and wife, Frank. And Mrs. Winter herself is not responsive. When I went to see her she was barely civil to me. A churlish sort of young woman I thought her. Though handsome in a peculiar style of course. Stay, what was that, Frank?" holding up her hand just as her son was about to speak.

They all listened. In the silence the sound Mrs. Carlyn had heard was becoming distinctly audible. Someone was running up the drive as if for dear life, more than one person apparently.

Carlyn got up. "Some one seems in a precious hurry. I think I will just go and see what they want."

He strolled towards the house. Moved by some sudden impulse Mrs. Carlyn and Barbara followed him. As they got nearer they saw that two men were running towards them at full speed, several more following in the distance.

"It is Jack Winter, sir," the first called out as he caught sight of the young squire. "He is dead!"

"Dead!" Carlyn's face turned a curious, greyish tint beneath its tan. "What do you mean, man? I parted from him only an hour ago."

"He is dead enough now, sir," panted the man whom Mrs. Carlyn recognized as Retford, one of the under-keepers. "Lying in a pool of blood in front of his cottage, shot through the head."

"Suicide!" Frank Carlyn drew in his breath sharply. "Spencer, I—"

"They are saying it's murder, sir," the man interrupted him respectfully.

"Good heavens!" Carlyn fell back a pace.

His mother touched his arm, her face white, her eyes big and frightened.

"Frank, what is it? Winter can't be dead. We were talking about him only this minute."

Carlyn put her aside hurriedly. "No, no! It is some stupid mistake of course. Probably the man has had a fit. You go into the house with Barbara, and I will run down to the cottage and see what really is the matter."

He scarcely waited for her answer as he hurried off to the gamekeeper's cottage. It was but a step away, as the North-country folk phrase it, when the near path through the Home Wood was taken, and Frank Carlyn was soon on the scene of action. Early as he was, however, quite a little crowd had assembled already.

Carlyn drew his brows together as he saw Marlowe, the village constable, officiously pushing the people aside and bending over something that lay on the ground.

The people, most of them his own employees, made way for the young squire. He glanced for a moment at the thing laying on the ground—the thing that so short a time before had been a living, breathing man—and turned away with a shudder of horror. The whole of the bottom part of the face had been blown away, and there were other ghastly injuries.

"Dead, poor fellow!" he said hoarsely.

The constable looked up. "As a door nail, sir. Whoever did this job didn't mean there to be any doubt about it."

Carlyn looked at him. "Whoever did it," he repeated. "But surely it is a clear case of suicide?"

The constable shook his head. "He couldn't have shot himself, sir, and then carried his gun off and thrown it behind that stack of wood, which is where Bill Jenkins found it just now. It's murder, safe enough, and here is Dr. Thompson to tell us all about it."

The doctor bustled up. He was a little, wiry man of sixty or thereabouts.

Motioning the bystanders away he knelt by the corpse. In a moment he looked up again.

"You are right, constable, there is nothing to be done here. We had better have him moved into the cottage. Tell his wife—but I will speak to her myself. Where is she?"

Constable Marlowe looked round. "Blest if I hadn't forgotten all about her," he ejaculated. "Where is she?"

Nobody answered for a minute. By one consent everybody turned and looked in at the cottage door, through which a glimpse could be obtained of the pleasant, homely interior. At last one man spoke:

"It was me that come on the body first, sir," he said slowly, addressing himself to Carlyn, his eyes wandering fearfully every now and then to that long, silent thing on the ground. "And as I come into the wood I met Winter's missus coming out. Tearing along like a wild thing she was, and never answered when I passed her the time of day civilly."

There was another silence. The bystanders looked at one another. Constable Marlowe drew a deep breath.

"Tearing along like a wild thing, was she? Phew!"

The inference was unmistakable. Frank Carlyn looked across at him with rising anger.

"What do you mean, Marlowe? Mrs. Winter has, no doubt, gone to see some of her friends and will be back presently. The tearing along was probably Spencer's fancy."

Spencer scratched his head.

"Beg pardon, sir, there was no fancy about it," he said stolidly. "And Jack Winter's missus has no friends hereabouts. Seems as if she thought no one good enough for her to associate with."

"Pooh! You are talking nonsense—" Carlyn was beginning, but Dr. Thompson touched his arm.

"Least said soonest mended," he said in a low tone. "We don't want to bring anyone's name into this. Come, they are going to take the poor fellow inside."

Winter's house was just the ordinary rural cottage, the front door led straight into the kitchen; opposite, another door led into the little parlour, a third opened on the closed stairs. There was a fire in the kitchen, a kettle was singing on the hob, a big black cat was curled up on the hearth, but of human presence there was no sign.

An odd expression flashed for a moment into Carlyn's eyes as he looked round. Was it relief, or was it fear? Dr. Thompson, who was watching his face narrowly, could not tell.

The men halted on the threshold with their burden. The doctor motioned them to the inner room, he and Carlyn following closely, Constable Marlowe bringing up the rear.

The principal piece of furniture in the room was a big, old-fashioned sofa. Here the bearers laid the dead man reverently. Frank Carlyn stood alone in the doorway while the doctor and the constable directed and helped the men. He looked swiftly round the room—a questioning, fearful glance—then he stepped quickly across to the fireplace, and from behind the cheap ornaments and shells with which it was adorned drew out a small, oblong object, and slipped it into his pocket.

He went back to the kitchen, and there presently Dr. Thompson and Marlowe joined him.

"That is all there is to be done for the present," the former said as he closed the door. "Except that the coroner must be communicated with."

Constable Marlowe looked at him. "Beg pardon, sir; there is another thing we have to do as quickly as possible, I think, and that is find Mrs. Winter. I am going to phone to headquarters at once, and I fancy you will find they will agree with me."

The doctor's kindly face over-clouded. "Oh, well, you may be right, Marlowe. But I hope Mrs. Winter will be at home very shortly and convince you that you are wrong."

"I don't fancy there is much chance of that, sir," the constable rejoined.

He wasn't an attractive man, Constable Marlowe, but his prominent jaw and his keen, deep-set eyes gave promise of a certain order of intelligence. The constable was by no means inclined to under-rate himself. He had made up his mind to rise in his calling, and had regarded it as little less than a calamity when he was sent to Carlyn village, which seemed to afford no scope for his ability. Now, however, with the mystery surrounding Winter's death, he told himself his opportunity had come. Rosy visions of a speedy promotion, of an inspectorship in the near future, even of a post in the detective force of the Metropolis dangled before his eyes. He watched the young squire and the doctor out of sight, and then went back into the cottage. A close study of the methods of Sherlock Holmes had taught him that the most unconsidered trifle would sometimes give the clue to the mystery. He did not intend that any such should escape the sharp eyes of Constable Marlowe.

Frank Carlyn returned to the hall. Dr. Thompson kept by his side; a great favourite of Mrs. Carlyn's, he knew he was assured of his welcome.

"This is a sad affair, a very sad affair," he remarked sympathetically.

Carlyn turned to him with something like passion in his tone.

"I tell you it is a case of suicide. I had just dismissed the man. Perhaps I had been unjustifiably harsh—"

The doctor shook his head. "Don't blame yourself, my dear Frank. This was no suicide. The shot was fired from some distance away. It would have been a physical impossibility for

Winter to have done it himself. As for what that fellow Marlowe was hinting at—well, poor young thing! Poor young thing! Heaven knows what she may have suffered at Winter's hands."

The view the doctor took of the case was unmistakable, but his pity for the young wife was so evidently genuine that some of the anger in Carlyn's face evaporated.

"I attended her in the spring," the doctor went on. "And I saw enough to know that some tragedy underlay the marriage. It was obvious, though she avoided all reference to the past, that she was of a very different class to her husband."

"Anyone could see that," Carlyn said gruffly. "But she had nothing to do with this, doctor."

"And yet," the doctor went on, "one of the things that struck me most was that there was nothing in the cottage, beyond its scrupulous cleanliness, no books, no knick-knacks or flowers to indicate that its mistress was a person of superior refinement."

"Wasn't there?" Carlyn's hand strayed to his breast pocket for an instant.

But, as the doctor went on with his surmises as to Mrs. Winter's origin, Carlyn's responses grew curter and curter. It was with a sigh of profound relief that when they reached the house, he deputed to Dr. Thompson the task of telling Mrs. Carlyn what had happened, and went off himself to his study.

He was still sitting there a couple of hours later when Constable Marlowe asked for an interview.

"We were right enough from the first, sir," he said when he was admitted. "Mrs. Winter had caught the 3.30 train up to town; when the inspector came he phoned up at once to have her stopped, but we were too late."

"How do you mean?" Carlyn's tone was stern. He shuffled the papers on his table as if to show the constable that he was wasting his time.

Marlowe coughed.

"We phoned to the junction, sir, but she wasn't in the train. She must have got out at Brentwood, the first stop. But we shall catch her soon, there is no doubt of that. The inspector is having her description circulated. But he is hampered in one way: there doesn't seem to be any photograph of her to be had. We were wondering if any of the servants up here would be likely to have one."

"I should think it was exceedingly unlikely," Carlyn's tone was short in the extreme. He rose to signify that the interview was ended. "But you must make what inquiries you like, constable. I think you are on the wrong track altogether, as you know."

"Yes, sir!" The constable's eyes gleamed unpleasantly. It was evident that he resented his dismissal. He glanced furtively round the room. "Time will show which of us is right, sir," he said as he left the room.

Left alone Frank Carlyn drew a small folding case from his pocket. It held three miniatures painted on ivory. One was that of a fine, soldierly-looking old man; opposite him a comparatively young woman with a sweet, serious face, and then, beneath, the lovely, laughing face of a very young girl with a mass of red-gold hair, and big, mischievous, grey eyes.

It was on this last that Carlyn's gaze was riveted.

"Yes, I was right to bring it, no one could have mistaken it," he said slowly.

With it in his hand he went slowly across to his writing-table, opened a drawer and thrust the miniature and case to the very back. Then he locked the drawer and thrust the key into his pocket, his face looking very grave and stern.

Chapter Two

"Castor is the next station, miss. The next stop I mean. You will have nearly an hour's run before you come to it." The speaker, a burly countryman, was following his family on to the platform and paused at the door to give this piece of information to the other occupant of the carriage, a tall woman in black sitting near the window at the other end.

"Thank you," she said with a slight bow. Touching his cap the man went on. The train began to move. The woman crossed over and opening her bag drew out a tiny pocket mirror. Holding it up she studied her face intently for a minute, then with a deep sigh she laid the glass back, replaced the smoke-tinted glasses she had momentarily taken off, and drew down her thick veil.

"It looks quite right," she said to herself in a low frightened whisper. "And it is so far away, surely there cannot be any danger."

She stood up and pulled down the shabby portmanteau with the letters E.B.M. stamped on one side. The label was addressed in firm angular writing—"Miss Elizabeth Martin, Davenant Priory, near Castor." She shuddered as she put it on the seat beside her. Then suddenly she burst into a passion of sobs.

"Oh, Lizzie, Lizzie, you were right, I can't do it," she cried. "And yet, God help me, what is to become of me if I don't?"

Her sobs subsided, she lay back in her seat, big tears coursing miserably down her cheeks. There was time to turn back yet, she said to herself, time to give up this mad scheme on which she had embarked. She knew that there was a door of escape open to her, but her pride and some feeling stronger than pride forbade her to avail herself of it. No; she told herself that there was nothing for it but to go forward in the path she had chosen; there could be no harm by it and at least she would be safe.

But all the while another voice was whispering to her, pleading with her to go back, to humble herself. When the train began to slow down she was still gazing mechanically out of the window, her expression strangely undecided.

"Castor! Castor!" the solitary porter the little station boasted shouted in stentorian tones.

Still for one second she sat motionless, then with a sudden look of resolution she got up, opened the door and stepped on to the platform.

There were a few passengers to get out at Castor. One trunk had already been hauled out of the van: "Miss Elizabeth Martin." She went up to claim it. An elderly woman was standing near it, an expression of perplexity on her comely face. She looked relieved as the passenger came up.

"Miss Martin, ma'am?" she said respectfully, then as the other murmured an inaudible assent she went on, "I'm Latimer, Lady Davenant's maid. Her ladyship desired me to see if I could help you in any way with your luggage. My lady intended coming to meet you herself, but she has one of her bad headaches this afternoon."

Miss Elizabeth Martin uttered a few words of polite regret and pulled her veil more closely down with fingers that visibly shook.

Latimer relieved her of her bag and wrap and led the way to a waiting motor-car.

Miss Martin glanced from side to side as they passed quickly down the narrow, little street. With its quaint black and white houses and pavements of cobble stones, Castor might certainly have passed for the original of Sleepy Hollow. Latimer pointed out the various objects of interest. The church, the Vicarage, the big old-fashioned market-place, the roof of Davenant Priory in the distance.

"'Tis but a bit of a walk," she said. "But folks are tired after a long journey, so her ladyship always has them met. Miss Maisie ought to have come with me, but she has never had a governess before and she is a bit frightened at the notion, so she ran away and curled herself up on Sir Oswald's sofa, and there isn't any of us dare fetch her away from there."

"Oh, dear! I do hope she won't be frightened at me," the new governess said with a touch of pathos in her tired tones. "I love children and I do want my little pupil to like me."

"She is bound to do that," Latimer said heartily, some motherly instinct in her touched by the appeal in the weary voice. She was wishing that Miss Martin would raise her veil or take off her disfiguring glasses. Latimer thought herself a good judge of faces, but she found herself baffled here. "Mrs. Sunningdale told her ladyship the gift you had with children was something wonderful," she concluded, as the car turned in at the entrance gates of the Priory.

The new governess shivered. "It is quite chilly here after town," she said as if in apology. "It was very kind of Mrs. Sunningdale to say that. I shall do my best to give satisfaction to Lady Davenant."

There was just a suspicion of hauteur in her tone, and Latimer drew back feeling vaguely rebuffed.

The door of the Priory stood hospitably open. The house itself was one of the oldest in the Midlands. In mediaeval days it had been famed as the home of godly and learned monks. At the time of the Reformation it had been too wealthy to escape the hand of the despoiler, and it and the broad lands pertaining to it had been bestowed by King Henry on one Thomas Davenant, just then the reigning favourite.

Since then the Davenants had prospered exceedingly. The second George had made the head of the family a baronet, and, though a course of gambling and cock-fighting had weakened the family exchequer, a couple of wealthy marriages in the nineteenth century had restored it to affluence.

The present owner was a widower with one small daughter, and his widowed mother presided over his establishment.

It was evident that Miss Elizabeth Martin was being treated with an unusual amount of consideration for a governess. She was escorted to her room by Latimer, who told her that her ladyship would see her when she had rested. A dainty tea was sent up to her, and then a smiling, white-capped maid appeared.

"If you will give me your keys, miss, I will put your things away," she said respectfully.

Miss Martin started violently. "Please don't trouble," she said hurriedly. "I would rather you did not. I always prefer to do my own unpacking."

The maid withdrew, rather aggrieved; then Elizabeth Martin stood up. She was still wearing the hat and coat in which she had travelled. Now she threw them aside and looked at herself in the pier-glass. She saw a tall, slim figure in an ill-made black gown, a small head well poised on a long slender throat, a quantity of hair that looked oddly dark against the clear, pale skin, that was brushed back sleek and straight and coiled in a hard and uncompromising knot on the nape of her neck. Near the temples a few stray locks seemed rebelling against their bondage, and inclined to curl themselves over her forehead. Damping a brush, she flattened them back. The smoke-coloured glasses hid her eyes; she pushed them further on as if anxious that they should shield her still more.

But when there was a knock at the door she was sitting prim and straight in her chair by the fireplace. "Her ladyship would like to see you now, ma'am, if you are rested," said the maid who had appeared before.

Miss Martin got up at once. "I am quite rested, thank you."

She followed the girl down what seemed to her an endless succession of steps and passages until at last the door was opened into a bright, prettily furnished room, and a cheerful voice bade them come in.

Lady Davenant was sitting in an easy-chair near the open window; a delicate-looking old lady. It was obvious that her headache was no fiction; she looked tired and languid in spite of a pleasant smile and a pair of big, dark eyes.

"I am so glad to see you, Miss Martin," she said, holding out a slender hand sparkling with jewels, and making the governess seat herself on the settee beside her. "I have heard so much of you from Mrs. Sunningdale that I feel we really are not strangers."

Miss Martin sat upright, her hands folded stiffly together on her lap.

"Mrs. Sunningdale was very good to me," she said slowly, with a faint quiver of the lips. "I hope I shall give you satisfaction, Lady Davenant, and so justify her kind recommendation of me."

Lady Davenant felt vaguely chilled. She had been certain of liking Miss Martin, Mrs. Sunningdale's enthusiasm about her had been quite infectious; she felt sure they had secured just the right person for Maisie, but now she began to wonder whether this grave, stiffly-spoken person would not depress her bright little grand-daughter.

"Mrs. Sunningdale was much disappointed you were not able to go back to India," she went on after a pause. "You had been three years with them, I think?"

The hands that lay on Miss Martin's knee were trembling in spite of her self-control.

"Three years," she assented in a low voice. "My health broke down then. My doctor told me it was hopeless to think of going out again."

"So I understand," Lady Davenant said sympathetically. "I hope you will soon get strong here in our pure country air."

"Oh, I am quite strong now, thank you," Miss Martin hastened to assure her. "It—it was only that India did not suit me. Am I to see my pupil to-night, Lady Davenant?"

Lady Davenant laughed a little. "Well, I really don't know. I am afraid Maisie has been terribly spoiled, Miss Martin. Her father lets her have her own way a great deal too much, but under present circumstances it is very difficult—I am sure Mrs. Sunningdale would explain to you—you know that your duties are not only confined to teaching Maisie, for the present at any rate."

"I know," Miss Martin assented gravely. "I am to read to Sir Oswald for some time every day; also to write his letters from his dictation."

"Yes." Lady Davenant acquiesced with a sigh. "Until recently we have had a distant cousin with us, Sybil Lorrimer, and she has managed everything for him, but she has been summoned away by the sudden illness of her father, so we want you to take her place. Sir Oswald's man is admirable in many ways, but my poor boy cannot endure his reading or his writing. You know that it is not a hopeless case, Miss Martin. The doctors say that there is very little doubt that Sir Oswald will recover his sight in time."

"Oh, I do hope so," Miss Martin said earnestly. "It must be so terrible to be blind."

"It is indeed! Especially for poor Oswald, who always hated inactivity. It is a year and a half since it happened. I know he often finds it almost unendurable. It was a terrible accident, the left wing of this house was on fire, and his wife was in her room overcome by the smoke. He had seen her out once, but she went back to fetch something. At first it seemed hopeless, but Oswald was like a madman, he would not believe that she could not be reached and he tied ladders together and insisted on going up himself. He reached her—oh, yes—but she was insensible, and he had to begin that terrible descent with a dead weight in his arms. The flames were pouring out of the lower story; they caught the ladder—it collapsed and brought them both to the ground. Poor Winifred was dead when they took her up, and Oswald was terribly injured; for weeks we despaired of his recovery, and when at last he did come back to life it was to find his sight gone, temporarily at any rate. Maisie was five and a half then—she is seven now—and the whole thing made a great impression on her. She is an extraordinarily sensitive child, and she is a great comfort to her father, so that I dare say you can understand she has been indulged. Not that I find any fault with her myself, she is a dear child. But Sybil said she was getting spoiled and that we ought to have a governess for her. Then we were fortunate enough to hear of you from Mrs. Sunningdale, and that is all, I think. Except about this afternoon. Maisie has taken it into her head to dislike the idea of a governess, and she has run away and hidden herself in her father's room, the one place where she knows she is safe, since no one ever disturbs her there."

"I quite understand," Miss Martin said slowly, though every nerve was a quiver. "But I think it will be all right. I generally get on with children, and I will do my best to give satisfaction to Sir Oswald."

"It is so little we can any of us do for him," Lady Davenant sighed. Then she glanced at the governess with kindly sympathy, "But I see you have had trouble too—you are in mourning. No near relative, I hope?"

Elizabeth Martin pressed her fingers together tightly.

"No relation at all," she said in a strained voice. "It was a very dear friend. But I generally wear black. I prefer it."

"Oh, do you?" Lady Davenant said hopelessly. She wanted to understand this young woman, to make her happy at the Priory, but she felt as though all her sympathy were being repelled, driven back upon herself. Then the sound of voices on the lawn outside made her turn her head.

"Ah, there is Maisie!" she exclaimed. "She is with her father. Come, Miss Martin. You can have your first look at your pupil unobserved."

Miss Martin got up and came to the window. She saw a tall, broad-shouldered man walking with wavering, uncertain steps and holding his hand, guiding him with all her small strength, a little, golden-haired child.

"She looks a dear little girl," the governess said, resting her hand heavily on the chair in front of her. "And it is very sad for Sir Oswald—terribly sad."

The words were commonplace enough, but the eyes behind the glasses were pitiful, the mobile lips were trembling.

Chapter Three

"And so the frog turned into a Prince, and married the Princess and they lived happily ever afterwards."

Elizabeth Martin's tone was very sweet and low, it had a tender inflection as she stroked the golden hair of the child who sat on a stool at her knee. The governess had been a week at the Priory now and Maisie had quite got over her aversion to the new order of things. She and her governess were the best of friends, but so far Miss Martin had seen nothing of Sir Oswald. It had been understood that she was to read to him and to write his letters, but so far apparently Sir Oswald was not inclined to avail himself of her services.

To-day, however, she had been told that he would be glad to see her in his study in half an hour's time, and she was feeling decidedly nervous at the prospect. She was beguiling the time by telling Maisie fairy tales. For the rest, she was settling down at the Priory. Maisie had proved amenable, as she had anticipated. Of Lady Davenant she saw little, often only meeting her at luncheon, but the old lady was kindness itself to her, and the old servants, and Latimer at their head, had apparently taken to her.

"I like that story," Maisie said in her pretty, decided tones when the story concluded. "Not so well as that about the Princess who became a swan, though. I told that to Daddy yesterday and he said it was very interesting."

"Did he?" Miss Martin said absently. Then she stood up. Maisie's words had brought her back to the realization of the present, had reminded her that the half-hour Sir Oswald's message had spoken of was nearly over. She went across to an oak-framed mirror that hung on the south wall, and glanced critically at herself in the glass. There was not a hair out of place on her dark, sleek head, her black gown with its plain white collar was as simple as any nun's. She turned and took Maisie's hand.

"Come, dear, we will go to the study now."

"Yes. And I will introduce you," Maisie laughed skipping along beside her. "Daddy said I was to. Do you know, Miss Martin"—her voice dropping to a confidential whisper—"I believe Daddy is a bit afraid of you. I do really. He said yesterday, 'I ought not to have let my mother make arrangements for me.' He said—"

"Maisie dear, don't you know that you must never repeat what people say?" Miss Martin's tone was not quite steady as she interrupted. She stopped a moment outside the study door, trembling nervously as though she could hardly bring herself to knock.

Maisie settled matters for her. With a joyous shout of "Daddy! Daddy! Miss Martin has come," she flung open the door and rushed in.

As Miss Martin hesitated on the threshold her eyes took in the whole scene. The room was pleasant and homelike enough, but there was something indescribably dreary and forlorn about the aspect of the man who sat in one of the big arm-chairs near the fireplace. There was hopeless dejection in the droop of the broad shoulders, in every line of the dark, rugged face.

Sir Oswald Davenant was not a handsome man. There was a certain virility about the large, roughly-hewn features and the forehead was broad and gave a promise of intellect, but there was a hint of weakness about the lower part of the face, in the lines of the mouth and the slightly receding chin. The deep-set eyes were hidden under heavy shades.

As Maisie spoke he half rose and held out his hand in an uncertain, tentative fashion.

"This is a very unceremonious introduction, Miss Martin," he said with a melancholy smile. "But I have heard so much about you from Maisie that I can hardly feel we are strangers. You have quite won the child's heart."

"You are very kind, Sir Oswald. Yes, Maisie and I are quite good friends," Miss Martin answered sedately as she lightly touched his proffered hand. "I understand you wish me to do some writing for you this morning."

Sir Oswald sank back heavily in his chair.

"If you will be so kind," he said wearily. "There is quite an accumulation over there. They should be stacked up in the rack."

He waited, one brown hand on the arm of his chair, while the governess went towards the table. He could hear her rustling among his papers and the sound fretted him almost past endurance. He hated to think that his correspondence was in the hands of a strange woman, and yet he could not help himself. Ever since Sybil went away he had been dependent on his man, and Perkins, though devoted to his master and excellent in his place, had his own notions both as to pronunciation and spelling and these had led to endless mistakes. In self-defence Sir Oswald had been obliged to fall back on the governess, who would at least be able to write decent English, he said to himself impatiently.

At last Miss Martin came back. "I have them all in order, I think, Sir Oswald," she said. "Some of them have been waiting several days, I see. If you will allow me I will read them to you, and make a note of the reply you wish sent."

"I shall be much obliged if you will," Sir Oswald said politely.

Maisie curled herself up on the rug at his feet. She was used to being quiet for hours when her father was absorbed in his troubles and disinclined to talk.

Miss Martin read out the letters in a clear, distinct voice. If it trembled occasionally, neither of her hearers noticed it.

Sir Oswald's replies were of the shortest. Most of his correspondence was of a business nature; one letter was redolent of perfume, breathed ardent wishes for his recovery, and spoke of the writer's speedy return. It was signed "Your affectionate cousin, Sybil Lorrimer."

Sir Oswald frowned when he heard it. Then he held out his hand.

"We will leave that for the present," he said as he put it in his pocket.

When she had finished, the governess rose.

"Now can I read to you, Sir Oswald? The papers, or a book?"

"Thanks, you are very good," Sir Oswald said wearily. "Yes, please, the papers. I may as well know what is going on in the world, even if I can take no share in it. As for books, I don't care for them. Unless I get hold of a good detective story. The tracing out of crime always has a curious fascination for me."

"How horrible!" The words seemed to burst from Miss Martin without her own volition. "I— I beg your pardon," she added, flushing. "I ought not to have said that, I—"

"I'm sure I don't know why you shouldn't," Sir Oswald said carelessly. "I don't expect everybody to share my opinions. I have sometimes thought that if I had been a younger son I should have been one of those police Johnnies myself. There was a case I was tremendously interested in last year. 'The Carlyn Wood Mystery' it was called in the papers. I wonder whether you remember it? But perhaps you were in India?"

"I—I think I remember it." Miss Martin's voice was trembling. She put one hand out and caught at the table beside her.

"A gamekeeper's wife murdered her husband and managed to make good her escape," Sir Oswald went on conversationally. "I was interested in it for two reasons, first because young Frank Carlyn was my fag at Eton, though I have seen nothing of him since, and secondly because of the mystery attaching to the unfortunate couple, the gamekeeper and his wife."

He paused as if waiting for some rejoinder, but the governess did not speak. The pallor of her cheeks had spread; now even her lips were white.

After a minute Sir Oswald went on:

"It was very odd altogether. It was said the wife, at any rate, belonged by birth to a superior position, but it was never really found out who either of them was. The man who gave Winter his reference was dead, and nothing could be discovered of the gamekeeper's career before he came to Mr. Carlyn. As for the wife, she seemed to vanish into thin air. A great many people appeared to sympathize with her, but I can't say I did. I should be delighted to hear of her capture. But I won't inflict any more horrors on you, Miss Martin"—for the governess had given a shiver of disgust and drawn a long breath that told its own story of distaste. "The Times leading articles, if you would be so good," he concluded, his momentary flash of interest dying out.

Miss Martin read very well, there could be no doubt of that. Her enunciation was clear and refined, the very opposite of Perkin's. Nevertheless she had only been reading a short time when Sir Oswald emitted an impatient sigh and began to stir about restlessly.

"I beg your pardon, Miss Martin," he said when she stopped. "You will think me an awful boor, but the fact is I can't get up any interest in any of these things. I was always an outdoor sort of man, don't you know! Thank you very much all the same."

Maisie uncurled herself and sprang up.

"Why don't you come out now, daddy?" she cried excitedly. "I am going to take Miss Martin to see the Wishing Well. And I will lead you, daddy, and Miss Martin will help. Do come!"

Sir Oswald gave a short, hard laugh. "You are promising a good deal for Miss Martin, childie. Looking after a blind man isn't such pleasant work. I assure you Perkins finds it no easy task."

"Oh, but we should like to help you, Maisie and I," Elizabeth Martin said impulsively. All the primness had gone out of her voice now, it was tremulous, soft, with a little quiver of pity running through.

Sir Oswald looked undecided. The air from the open window was blowing upon him, it felt warm and balmy, the call of the spring was upon him. His enforced inaction, the confinement indoors, were irksome to him. Yet he seemed to have none of the resources of blind folks. He lived in the hope of the restoration of sight which the doctors promised him. It was scarcely worth while to exert himself, when, as he expected, his period of idleness would soon be over. In the meanwhile he hated being driven; walking, which he had previously loved, was a very different affair when it could only be undertaken with the aid of Perkins's arm. It often ended in Sir Oswald's remaining in the house for days, except for a little stroll with Maisie in the grounds immediately in front of the house. But to-day the mention of the Wishing Well called up memories of his boyish days, of the time when he had believed that if you wished as you drank from the old well your wish was certainly granted. A longing came over him for the green freshness of the woods, for a draught of the ice-cold water.

"If you will really be so good, Miss Martin," he said at last.

Maisie clapped her hands with delight. Sir Oswald scarcely had time to change his mind, for it did not take either Miss Martin or her charge long to get ready and they all set off down the drive together.

Maisie held her father's hand and guided him, Miss Martin keeping a watchful eye on both. As far as the lodge it was familiar ground to Sir Oswald, he managed fairly well, but once inside the Fount Wood where the Wishing Well was situated it was a very different matter. The soft, mossy path was worn and uneven; bare old tree roots stretched across it, long outstanding branches caught the passers by. Sir Oswald stumbled more than once.

Elizabeth Martin came to his right side. "Let me help you, Sir Oswald, as well as Maisie." She drew his arm through hers, and walked carefully, guiding him past the difficult bits.

Sir Oswald was inwardly calling himself a fool for coming. Yet as his hand rested on the governess's rounded arm, as she talked quietly of the scenery of which she caught glimpses through the openings in the trees, he grew interested in identifying the various landmarks from her descriptions. It was curious, too, how she seemed to divine just what he would like to know—how the young larches were doing at the end of the plantation, and how the wood looked where they were thinning out the timber. He grew quite interested at last, her answers were so intelligent, so unlike Perkins, "Getting a bit thin like, Sir Oswald," or "Looking fresh like, Sir Oswald."

He was surprised to find how short the walk had seemed when they reached the Wishing Well. They all sat down on the big flat boulders near the mouth. But out of doors Maisie was never quiet long. She began to dance about, dipping her little hands in the clear, limpid water.

"You must drink, Miss Martin," she ordered excitedly. "And you must wish as you drink. Then if you don't tell anybody it's sure to be granted."

The governess smilingly obeyed Maisie's instructions to make a hollow of her palm and stooped towards the well. Then as she bent her head her glasses tipped forward, she caught ineffectually at them, and they fell off on to the moss at her feet. She uttered a quick exclamation of dismay as she reached after them and the water in her hand splashed unheeded down her dress.

Maisie cried out in vexation. "There, you have spilt the water, Miss Martin, and it means bad luck, for you can't draw water from the well twice in one day, so now you can't wish. And all because of those stupid, old spectacles. And you look ever so much nicer without them. She has such pretty grey eyes, daddy, just like Mummy's."

"Maisie, do you know that you haven't wished yourself yet?" Sir Oswald interrupted. "Come, little girl, you must make haste, I can't stay here too long."

Maisie darted off. Her quickened breathing told Sir Oswald that Miss Martin was near.

"It was strange that Maisie should say your eyes were like her mother's," he said in a low tone. "For I have thought once or twice this afternoon that your voice reminded me of hers—my wife's— I have wondered whether there might be any relationship?"

"Quite impossible," Miss Martin said coldly. "I have no relations." Her hands were clasping one another tightly, the fingers were interlacing themselves.

"Still, perhaps—" Sir Oswald was beginning when there was an interruption.

Down the mossy path by which they had come a dainty figure was tripping lightly.

With a cry Maisie sprang forward. "Cousin Sybil!"

Miss Lorrimer's golden hair shone in the sunlight, her pretty red lips were smiling as her big, blue eyes glanced round the little group.

"Mrs. Barnes at the lodge told me you had come this way," she said as she kissed Maisie and let her hand rest on Sir Oswald's shoulder. "So I thought I would come after you. I am so glad I did. And now, Maisie," her eyes resting questioningly on the stranger, a shade of harshness creeping into the honeyed tones, "this lady I suppose is your new governess, Miss Martin."

Chapter Four

"I don't trust her," Sybil Lorrimer said, as she caught up a feather fire-screen and held it between her face and the flames. "Miss Martin looks to me like a woman with a secret, a woman with a past."

"Oh, my dear!" Lady Davenant spoke reproachfully. Sybil had followed her into the morning-room. "I really think you have taken a causeless prejudice against the poor girl. She seems so nice and unassuming and quiet, and I am sure if there had been anything of that kind Mrs. Sunningdale would not have recommended her to me."

"Perhaps she didn't know," Sybil said carelessly. She was thinking that if Mrs. Sunningdale was at all like her friend, Lady Davenant, it would be no difficult matter to deceive her.

Miss Lorrimer's unexpected visit to the Priory had lasted over a week, but her father had had a relapse, and she was urgently wanted at home. She was returning the next day. It was easy to see that the summons was unwelcome. Sybil's face wore an impatient frown, she was tapping her foot restlessly on the floor.

"What do you know of Miss Martin before she went to Mrs. Sunningdale?" she asked after a pause.

"I forget," Lady Davenant said vaguely. "Oh, I believe she had been with some one in the country—a doctor's family I think it was—but I don't remember the particulars. Perhaps I could find Alice Sunningdale's letter, Sybil. But I know she spoke most highly of Miss Martin."

"Yes," Sybil said slowly, her white fingers toying with the screen as she laid it down in her lap and gazed reflectively at the fire. "But, after all, it was only a written reference, wasn't it? I wish Mrs. Sunningdale were in England, it would be much more satisfactory if one could see her."

"Really Sybil, I think you are talking very absurdly!" Lady Davenant said with sudden fire. "I'm quite satisfied with Miss Martin and I do not know what fault you have to find with her." She drew her writing-case towards her as she spoke and began to search through the various papers it contained.

"I thought I had put Alice Sunningdale's letter here, but at any rate this is the second one she wrote—just before she sailed," she announced at last.

"Listen, Sybil:

My dear Lady Davenant,

I cannot tell you how glad I am to hear that you have engaged my friend, Miss Martin, for after her kindness to me and the children out in Blondapore when little Frank was born I have looked upon her entirely as a friend, not a governess. I am sure you will find her all you need for Maisie, and a sweet, sympathetic companion for Sir Oswald and yourself. I envy you really—if only her health had allowed her to come out with us we should never have parted with her. I do wish I had time to run down to the Priory to see you all before we sail, but it is impossible. Good-bye, dear Lady Davenant, kindest remembrance to Sir Oswald and love to Maisie and yourself.

Ever yours,

ALICE SUNNINGDALE.

"There now, could anything be more satisfactory?" Lady Davenant concluded in a tone of triumph as she finished the letter.

"It certainly seems everything you could wish," Sybil assented thoughtfully.

She stood up and, leaning against the high, carved mantelpiece, drew her foot in its little buckled shoe backwards and forwards over the brass fender-rail.

"Where are the Sunningdale children at school?" she asked at last.

Lady Davenant looked relieved, taking it for granted, good, easy soul, that Sybil's doubts had been set at rest by the perusal of the letter.

"The two eldest are in Switzerland somewhere," she answered. "Then they lost several, you know, and the two youngest went back with their mother to India."

Sybil did not answer. Apparently she had had enough of the subject. Her brows were drawn together in a frown as she watched the flickering firelight reflected in her buckles.

She had sense enough to see that it was useless to think of influencing Lady Davenant against Miss Martin, unless she had something definite to bring against the governess, but her determination to get rid of this interloper at the Priory grew and strengthened.

Sybil Lorrimer was the daughter of a half-pay Colonel. From her earliest years she had known the grind of poverty, and as soon as she could think for herself she had made up her mind to take the earliest opportunity of escaping from it. Unfortunately such opportunities did not seem to come her way. She was undeniably pretty, but the hoped-for wealthy suitors did not present themselves, and at four and twenty Sybil Lorrimer was inclined to write herself down among the failures. Then at last fortune had favoured her. She had been included in the house-party at the Priory at the time of young Lady Davenant's death, and the relationship between them, slight as it was, had afforded her a pretext for offering to stay with Sir Oswald's mother during those first days of bereavement.

From that day Sybil had never wavered in the path she had marked out for herself. She meant to marry Sir Oswald Davenant and take her share of the pleasant things of life. Whether he recovered his sight or not mattered little to her. To be called Lady Davenant and to have practically unlimited wealth at her command was all that counted. Up to three months ago she had felt assured of success, she had read to Sir Oswald and talked to him. It had seemed to her that he was growing more and more dependent upon her, then suddenly his manner changed; he set up, as it were, a barrier between them.

Unable to believe that the cause of failure lay in herself, Sybil had at last come to the conclusion that Maisie was the obstacle. Maisie was always in her father's room, always putting her oar in their conversation.

Sybil it was who had impressed upon Lady Davenant the necessity for getting a governess for Maisie, who had declared that left to her nurse's care Maisie was getting spoilt and unmanageable.

She had not dreamed that the governess would see anything of Sir Oswald at all, she had merely looked upon her as a buffer to keep Maisie out of the way.

But Sybil had not reckoned upon being absent when the governess came, least of all had she expected to find Miss Martin installed as Sir Oswald's amanuensis. Now she had to confess that the governess was a much greater hindrance to her plans than Maisie had ever been. She had tried to take her old place, to manage her cousin's correspondence for him, only to find herself politely but quietly repulsed.

She had no idea how her tinkling jewellery, and her rather shrill voice and affected manner had got on Sir Oswald's nerves, how restful he found the sweet voice and low tones of the woman who had taken her place.

But Sybil saw plainly that her scheme was within an ace of failure, that unless something should drive Elizabeth Martin from the Priory she must certainly look for defeat. That it was inevitable in any case, that Sir Oswald himself had seen through her plans and quietly frustrated them, she did not guess. All her thoughts were concentrated on getting rid of the governess, but the effort did not promise to be as easy of fulfilment as she had anticipated.

Lady Davenant had proved difficult to manage. It looked pretty hopeless from Sybil's point of view, and her heart sank as she thought of the possible downfall of the brilliant future she had built in the air, of her return to poverty and disappointment.

She left Lady Davenant and went back to her own room.

The governess, for her part, could not help being conscious of the scarcely veiled hostility of Miss Lorrimer's attitude towards her. In vain she tried to placate her. She saw that her efforts were in vain, and, though for the most part she told herself that she was too insignificant to be taken seriously by Lady Davenant's cousin, there were times when she feared that Sybil's dislike might prove a very real source of danger.

That night she went up early to her room, and, when she had slipped into her dressing-gown and let down her hair, she unlocked her box and took out an inlaid casket of Eastern design, with queer old dragons with gilded bodies and wicked jewelled eyes sprawling all over it, and a lock of intricate and delicate make. Opening it, she drew out a packet of old papers and letters, then seating herself in the easy chair by the fireplace she began to read, burning each sheet as she finished it. She was nearing the end of the bundle when there was a sharp, hurried knock at the door.

She did not answer, but her hands dropped on her lap as if paralysed, she sat and stared at the door. For once the disfiguring glasses had been thrown aside and a pair of big, grey eyes, fringed by dark, upcurled lashes, looked out from the heavy mass of dark hair which clung round her forehead. The knocking came again, louder and more insistent.

With a gesture of despair she half rose to her feet, then clasping her hands round her slender throat she fell back in her chair.

The knocking went on, the door handle was turned noisily, through the thick old oak she caught the sound of a voice.

"Miss Martin!"

Some of the fear died out of the grey eyes now, she looked at the letters she still held, then she threw them quickly into the fire and sprang up.

"What is it? Who is there?" she called, and her clear tones were as steady as usual.

"It is I—Sybil Lorrimer!" The answer came as the handle was again turned ineffectually. "Let me in. I am frightened."

Miss Martin unlocked the door. "What is the matter?"

Sybil threw the door open and hurried in.

"Oh, I have been terrified," she shivered. "Somebody is trying to break into the house by the windows beneath mine. I heard some sounds and looked out and saw a dark figure. Ugh! I was frightened. I tore out of the room. I don't think I stopped running until I got here."

Sybil's breath came quick and fast, she held her hand pressed to her side, but her keen eyes were taking in every detail of the room. They wandered from the startled eyes of the woman before her to the charred ashes on the hearth, to the half burned paper in the fire.

Their gaze reminded Elizabeth that she was comparatively defenceless without her glasses. She turned aside quickly and caught them up. As she adjusted them she turned her back to Sybil, and that young lady, coming nearer, noted with malicious satisfaction that the thick, dark hair curling over the governess's shoulders was of a distinctly different hue near the roots.

But the idea of a man trying to get into the house was alarming. Elizabeth, too, was pale as she hastily twisted up her hair.

"Ought we not to give the alarm, rouse the servants—Sir Oswald?" she questioned.

"Yes! Yes!" Sybil gripped her arm. "Still, of course poor Oswald is no use and we ought not to alarm Lady Davenant.

But we must be very quiet or they will get away. You come to my room with me and see if we can make out exactly what they are doing, and then we will call the men."

Elizabeth crossed the room and poked the remains of the paper well into the fire, then she said slowly:

"Yes, I will come with you. But I should have thought an alarm bell—"

"Don't I tell you it would alarm the burglars, as well as frighten Lady Davenant out of her wits?" Sybil said impatiently. Glancing round she had seen a tiny object on the floor that made her doubly anxious to get the other girl out of the room. She almost dragged the governess with her. "Quick! Quick!" she panted. "They may be inside now."

Elizabeth had no idea where Miss Lorrimer's room was, and Sybil gave her little time to notice the geography of the house. She literally pushed her up and down stairs and along passages, and at last threw open a door. She drew Elizabeth across to the window.

"Listen!" she whispered.

Elizabeth listened intently, but not a sound did she hear.

"They must be inside," Sybil said in a low voice. "Wait, you stay here and watch. I will rouse Walters and the footmen."

She darted away, and before Elizabeth had quite realized her intention had hurried out of the room.

Left alone, the governess devoted her attention to the window. She could not hear the slightest sound of any description, the window apparently overlooked the terrace, but as she peered out the thought crossed her mind to wonder how in the darkness Sybil had contrived to see the form she had described.

Meanwhile Miss Lorrimer had not gone straight to the servant's quarters, she had made a little detour which took her round by Miss Martin's room. Her sharp eyes had noticed a tiny packet that had slipped unseen beside Elizabeth's chair. She ran across the room and picked it up, assuring herself by a glance that Elizabeth had taken care that no scrap of paper was left large enough to be intelligible.

To undo the packet was the work of a second. A tiny curl of red-gold hair clung round her finger, labelled "Baby Rosamond." Beside it there was a photograph of a dark, rather coarse-looking man. It was on this that Sybil's gaze was riveted.

It was unexpectedly familiar, and yet she could not place it. "Now where in the world," she cogitated, "can I have seen that face before?"

Chapter Five

"LADY DAVENANT wishes me to dine to-night."

"So do I," Sir Oswald said with a smile. The delicate colour that the fresh air of Davenant had brought to Elizabeth's cheeks deepened a little. She was sitting in her accustomed place at Sir Oswald's writing-table. Sir Oswald was leaning back in one of the big easy chairs near the window.

Elizabeth got up and came over to him.

"Well, I don't know that it is very good for Maisie to sit up so late, but of course Lady Davenant's wishes and yours are paramount."

"Especially mine." He laughed whimsically. He was looking infinitely brighter than in the days when Sybil Lorrimer was acting as his secretary. He was growing more exacting in his demands on Miss Martin's time, too, and Maisie often had an unexpected holiday. To-day the Rector and his wife were dining at the Priory. They were bringing an old friend who was staying. Maisie was a great favourite of theirs, they had begged that she might dine, and Lady Davenant had made a special point of Miss Martin's accompanying her pupil.

It was the first time such an occasion had arisen since her coming to the Priory, and the governess would have done much to avoid it. This, however, was impossible in the face of Lady Davenant's wishes, and she perforce had to resign herself to the inevitable.

Sybil Lorrimer was still away. Her father had died a couple of days after his relapse, and there had been much to arrange. It was understood, however, that Miss Lorrimer was returning to the Priory as soon as possible to pay a long visit and to recruit her health after the strain through which she had passed. Nerves were supposed to have been the cause of the burglar scare, for the strictest search had failed to reveal any trace of nocturnal intruders. Nothing of value was missing. Elizabeth alone had lost a tiny parcel. She had come to the conclusion, after much vain searching and many tears, that in the hurry and excitement of Sybil's entrance she must have thrown it into the fire with the papers.

Elizabeth was twisting her fingers about nervously. Some sixth sense told the blind man opposite that she was in trouble.

"What is it?" he asked quietly. "Is it anything I can do for you?"

"Yes, I think so." Elizabeth's lips were trembling. It was obvious that she was speaking only under the stress of some strong emotion. "It is—Sir Oswald—Lady Davenant has asked me to sing to-night. And I can't—I can't—to-night."

"To sing," Sir Oswald repeated, his dark face softening. "But don't you know that I want to hear you—that it was at my suggestion that my mother asked you? I know that you must sing divinely—I can hear it in your voice, and can't you guess what music is to a blind man?"

"Ah, yes!" There was a little sobbing quiver in the girl's voice now. "And another time I will sing to you as much as you like, but not to-night—not to-night. Won't you help me?"

There was a momentary pause. Then Sir Oswald said gently:

"Of course you shall not sing if you would rather not. But is it a promise? Will you sing to me another day?"

"Yes, yes!" Elizabeth said feverishly. "Any other time that you like."

Sir Oswald rose and stretched out his hand.

"That is a bargain, then." He held her slim, cool fingers in his a moment. "Why, surely you know I—we would not ask you to do anything that would cause you pain?"

The governess drew her hand away decidedly.

"You and Lady Davenant are always very kind to me," she said stiffly. "Is that all, Sir Oswald? I have finished the letters and I have to dress."

"Pray do not let me detain you. I am sure you must be tired. I am much obliged for your kind help," Sir Oswald said courteously. His tone was perceptibly colder. It was evident that he had felt the rebuff.

Elizabeth stood a moment, her colour flickering, her lips parted as though she was about to speak, then her hands dropped to her side, she turned and left the room.

She hastened upstairs. On the bed was laid out the one evening dress she possessed. It was not in any sense a fashionable one, it was too long in the sleeves and too high in the neck, but it was better made than most of her garments and fitted her tall, slim figure to perfection. When it was donned, she looked at herself with dissatisfied eyes, then she put on her smoked glasses and gave a sigh of relief. "That is better."

As she turned to leave the room a sudden vision of the last time she had dined late rose before her eyes and filled them with hot, scorching tears. She saw again the big dining-room, the exquisitely appointed table, above all the kind, smiling eyes of the father who had loved her, whose pride she had been. She heard her own voice.

"So Céleste has done my hair in the newest fashion, daddy. Don't I look grown up?"

"Ah, but I don't want my little girl turned into a grown-up woman," her father had returned with a gay laugh. It was the last time his eyes had smiled at her, the last time she had been "Daddy's little girl."

It was just ten years ago to-night. As she thought of the father whose grey hair had gone down in sorrow to his grave she bent her head for a moment over her clasped hands, then Maisie's voice was heard outside. Elizabeth dashed the tears from her eyes. She was the governess again, nothing more.

Maisie was much excited at the prospect of dining down-stairs. The guests, the rector and his wife and their visitor, had already arrived. Maisie hurried off to greet her friends. The governess slipped quietly into a seat half shadowed by the heavy window curtains.

Then she glanced round the room.

Sir Oswald was talking to Mrs. Stamways, the rector's wife, and his face wore the look of sadness that was becoming habitual to it. Elizabeth looked in vain for the rare smile that at times transformed his whole expression.

"So I hear you are a stranger in the neighbourhood, like myself."

The voice made Elizabeth start; she looked up quickly. The Stamways' guest had come over to her corner and was taking a seat near.

She was a pleasant-looking woman, still in the early forties. Her dark hair was powdered with grey, but her complexion was as fresh, her eyes as bright as those of a young girl. Voice and manner were alike pleasant, and Elizabeth felt strangely drawn to her.

"I am thinking of taking a house in the neighbourhood for the summer," she went on conversationally. "Walton Grange. I wonder if you know it?"

"I don't think so," Elizabeth said doubtfully.

"Ah, well! You will have to bring Maisie to see me when I am settled there," the other said quickly. "It is quite an Elizabethan house, you know—a moat and all that sort of thing."

They went on talking. Lady Davenant was talking over parish matters with Mrs. Stamways. Sir Oswald and the rector were discussing the political prospects, Maisie was occupying the attention of the only other visitor—the curate.

When dinner was announced, Elizabeth felt that she had made a friend, and she looked forward eagerly to a renewal of the conversation.

"I think I shall have to take you in, Miss Martin," said Maisie, offering her little arm gravely as the others paired off.

At the dinner table Elizabeth found herself between Maisie and Mr. Meyer, the curate, while opposite she could catch a glimpse of her new friend talking to Sir Oswald.

For some time the conversation was general, but at last there came a lull.

Sir Oswald was speaking.

"Yes, Walton Grange is a delightful old house. A trifle gloomy, perhaps, and I hope you won't find it dull in the neigh-bourhood, Lady—" Elizabeth did not catch the name. "I don't know whether Walton is quite the house for a lady living alone."

"Oh, but I think I shall not be alone long," his partner inter-rupted him with the flashing smile Elizabeth found so delightful. "I hope later on to have my daughter with me."

"Oh, you have a daughter, I beg your pardon, but I had no idea—" Sir Oswald said with a puzzled air.

"She has been away from home so long that, like the rest of the world, you have forgotten," she interrupted him, and it seemed suddenly that her mouth and eyes grew sad. "But I naturally remember, and I do not think it will be long before she comes home now. And then you see I shall not find Walton Grange gloomy, and I shall not mind your neighbourhood being dull, because I shall have my girl at home again."

"But surely—" Elizabeth did not catch the rest of Sir Oswald's rejoinder.

Quite a hubbub of conversation seemed to rise around and she heard no more.

But as she listened and replied to the curate's mild platitudes, she could not help thinking of the sweet-faced woman opposite and wondering what the daughter could be like who apparently of her own free choice left such a mother to solitude. She looked again at the kind eyes and the tender mouth, and a sudden swift longing that she had known such a mother came over her. Surely then she would have been guarded and protected, and she would not have made havoc with her life.

Meanwhile the curate was thinking that Miss Martin was even more difficult to talk to than he had imagined. When he first spoke to her she seemed to look right over his head and replied to his remarks most diconcertingly at random. Those smoked spectacles, too, were a tremendous drawback, he decided; it was like talking to some one on the other side of a screen or down the telephone, an instrument which Mr. Meyer frankly detested.

Yet as she turned to speak to Maisie, he could not help admiring the delicate profile, the dainty moulding of chin and throat, and wishing that he could see her eyes behind the glasses. He rather admired the straight, plain bands of hair, they reminded him of the Madonnas of the early Masters.

He went on talking, perhaps in time she would become more responsive, he hoped. Presently the subject of the Stamways' guest and Walton Grange occurred to him.

"It is a lonely old place," he prattled on. "The grounds are extensive, and there are quaint yew hedges with birds and beasts carved on the top, don't you know. But I should not care for the moat myself. I should fancy it would make a house damp. Perhaps I am rather inclined to exaggerate that danger, though," he added with the little laugh which Elizabeth thought so affected, "since rheumatism is a terrible complaint in my family."

"Indeed! That is very sad," Elizabeth said politely.

"Yes! It is a cruel infliction," Mr. Meyer went on. "Not of course that there are not many worse," he added in his clerical manner, "from which we must be thankful we do not suffer. Lady Treadstone will be an acquisition to the neighbourhood, I am sure."

"Lady—who?"

The question broke across his halting sentences like a bombshell.

If Mr. Meyer had sought to obtain Miss Martin's attention his words had certainly had the desired effect now. The governess's cheeks, even her lips were white. It was evident that she was suffering from some almost uncontrollable agitation.

"Lady—who?" she repeated feverishly. "What—name did you say? Not—"

Mr. Meyer looked at her, his mild blue eyes wide with amazement.

"Treadstone," he said again. "Why, Miss Martin, surely you knew that the lady to whom you were talking so long before dinner was Lady Treadstone?"

"No, I did not know," Elizabeth said dully. A great mist was rising before her eyes, she felt suddenly faint and sick, she bit her lips, she dug her nails deep in the palms of her hands. At all hazards she must not, dare not, faint.

"She is the late Lord Treadstone's widow," Mr. Meyer went on. "And of course he was immensely rich, he left everything he could away from the title to her. I did not know she had a daughter, but I expect it would be by her first marriage. She was a widow when she met Lord Treadstone."

"Was she?" For the life of her Elizabeth could say no more. It was with unfeigned relief that she saw Lady Davenant give the signal to leave the table.

As she followed the others into the drawing-room she saw Lady Treadstone make room for her on the settee, she saw the other woman's kind eyes cloud over as she passed on coldly and placed herself behind Lady Davenant.

The evening seemed interminable to her, but it was not in reality long before Lady Davenant signed to her that she and Maisie might retire. She would have passed out with a slight bow, but Lady Treadstone rose.

"Our little chat has made me feel we ought to know one another better, Miss Martin," she said pleasantly. "Will you drive over with me and look at Walton one day next week? It would give me so much pleasure."

Elizabeth constrained herself to answer coldly, more than ever thankful for the screen that hid the passion in her eyes.

"You are very kind. But my time is not my own."

"I am sure Lady Davenant—" Lady Treadstone said eagerly.

But Elizabeth only bent her head. "I fear it would be quite impossible, thank you very much."

Upstairs in her room she dashed the glasses from her eyes, she threw back her masses of hair.

"Did she know me?" she asked herself wildly. "My God, is it possible she knew me?"

Chapter Six

SIR OSWALD DAVENANT was walking up and down his study. Long familiarity with the accustomed furniture had made him able to do so with comparative impunity, though every now and then he caught his foot against something and cursed the blindness that impeded his movements.

He was doing the one thing he had hitherto believed impossible to him, the one thing that had had no place in his well-regulated existence—he was falling in love.

His marriage had been very happy, he had been very fond of Winifred, the boy and girl friendship had ripened into a very real affection, but there had been—as he himself would have phrased it—"no nonsense about it."

This was a very different thing, this craving for the voice and hands of the woman he had never seen. He told himself that the blindness was at fault over this, too, and to some extent he was right. Had he been living his usual active, outdoor life, Elizabeth Martin might have remained his child's governess to him and nothing more. But, as it was, he caught himself longing for her step in the passage, like the veriest love-sick boy. At first he had not quite realized what it meant, but the hour for deceiving himself was over; to-day for the first time he was asking himself what was to be the end of it all.

He had always made up his mind that if he recovered his sight he would marry again; he wanted a mistress for his house, a son, an heir to his title and estates. But he had always pictured himself looking round among the marriageable ladies of his acquaintance and choosing a wife with as much thought and deliberation as he gave to all the weightier things of life. Falling suddenly in love had had no place in his calculations.

He had not arrived at any satisfactory conclusion when there was a perfunctory tap at the door, and Sybil Lorrimer entered hurriedly.

"Aunt Laura"—she had expressed a wish to call Lady Davenant by this name lately—"has had a letter from Barbara. She is staying with the Turners at Ipsford, with her fiancé, and she is going to bring him over for inspection one of these fine days."

"I am glad of that," Sir Oswald said heartily. "I shall be delighted to renew my acquaintance with Barbara. She is a good girl and deserves one of the best."

"Certainly she does," Sybil acquiesced, but there was not much warmth in her tone.

Her blue eyes were watching Sir Oswald very narrowly. She saw that he was restless, listening, and her face darkened. She was looking her best in her new mourning, not that that mattered to Sir Oswald, as she said to herself gloomily. But its dead black enhanced the fairness of her skin, the gold of her hair, the blue of her eyes. There was a becoming flush on her cheeks now. She went round to the writing-table.

"Any letters I can write, Oswald? I see Miss Martin has been busy already." A faint sneer was in her voice. "What a paragon that woman is!"

"Miss Martin is most kind and valuable," Sir Oswald said stiffly.

There was an accent of defence, of possession almost in his tone that made Sybil feel as if another nail had been driven into the coffin that held her dead hopes. Instinct told her that it would be wise to be silent, but the desire to implant a sting was too strong for her.

"I am sure she is," she assented. "Nevertheless, I wish you could see her, Oswald, I wish your eyes were open, my dear cousin," she ended with a stifled sob.

Oswald felt supremely uncomfortable. Little as he cared for Sybil Lorrimer, she had been kind to him in the early days of his blindness. He had no wish to appear ungrateful. Nevertheless the slighting tone in which she habitually spoke of Elizabeth Martin grated upon him now, as always.

"I certainly wish I could see Miss Martin or anyone," he said, after a moment's pause. "But, Sybil—I had not meant to mention it to you or anyone yet, but I think I must make you an exception—I went over to Saltowe last week and paid Dr. Maitland a visit."

"Yes?" questioned Sybil eagerly.

"He says that I have made wonderful progress in the past two months; he wants to take me up to Town to see Sir William Chandler next week, then, if he is satisfied, a slight operation would have to be performed. I should have to go into a nursing home for a few days, and then, Maitland says, it would be a practical certainty that I should see all right again."

"Oh, how glad I am for your sake!" Sybil exclaimed. She took his hand and held it a minute between her soft palms. "This is the best news in the world."

"Thank you very much," Sir Oswald said, trying to speak unconstrainedly, as, after giving her hand a cousinly pressure, he contrived to free his own.

Sybil was busy with speculations as to how this intelligence would affect her. She did not doubt that it would effectually put an end to Miss Martin's rivalry. No man with the use of his eyes could hesitate between her and the dowdy-looking governess, she agreed. Besides, the passing of Sir Oswald's blindness would necessarily imply the close of his association with Miss Martin.

She would be relegated to her proper place, Sybil said to herself viciously. Still, there remained the society round, into which an eligible parti such as Sir Oswald Davenant would be eagerly welcomed. Sybil decided that it behoved her to lose none of the time remaining.

"Won't you come out for a walk this lovely morning?" she said. "Do, Oswald. It would do you good."

He hesitated.

"Well, Miss Martin and Maisie have gone down to Dr. Williams with a message. I promised to walk as far as the lodge to meet them. If you will be my escort instead of Perkins, I shall be most grateful."

Sybil's brows were drawn together. She bit her underlip. This was not at all what she had meant, but she told herself she could not afford to refuse.

"Of course I shall be delighted," she returned. "I won't be a moment putting on my hat, Oswald."

She was back almost as soon as she had promised, and they set off down the drive, Sybil exerting herself to keep up the inconsequent chatter which she fancied amused Sir Oswald. His attention wandered considerably, and she received some vague replies for which, perhaps unjustly, she blamed the governess, and which had the effect of renewing her wrath against that luckless individual.

They had nearly reached the lodge gate when they caught sight of the two coming towards them. Warm though the day was, Miss Martin still wore her thick veil and her horn-rimmed glasses.

Maisie greeted the new-comers joyfully and at once attached herself to her father. Sir Oswald dropped Sybil's arm.

"I think my daughter will be my guide," he said playfully.

Sybil had to acquiesce with a smile, but she was by no means rendered more amiable. She glanced at the governess, who was walking silently at Maisie's side.

"How do you contrive to bear that thick veil this weather, Miss Martin! I should simply faint if I tried to walk about in one."

The attack was unexpected. The governess flushed hotly.

"I am used to it. I do not find it too hot," she hesitated. Then her voice steadied itself. "I first took to it because I have very bad neuralgia in my temples, and when one has accustomed oneself to anything of this kind it is very difficult to leave it off."

"So I should imagine," said Sybil disagreeably.

They walked on a few steps, then Elizabeth turned to Sir Oswald.

"I wonder whether I might leave Maisie with you for a few minutes, Sir Oswald? I have a message from Dr. Williams for Lady Davenant and I should like to deliver it as soon as possible."

"By all means," Sir Oswald assented courteously. "We can't wander very far, Miss Martin. You will find us somewhere about here when you come back."

"Thank you very much," the governess responded. She walked on briskly, her tall, slight figure looking brisk and alert as it was outlined against the grey old trunks of the oaks in the drive.

"Miss Martin did not like what you said about her veil," Maisie said shrewdly. "Did you want to, make her cross, Sybil?"

It was Sybil's turn to flush now. "No, of course I didn't," she said irritably. "But I can't think of why she wears the thing. It's just as though she were afraid of her face being seen."

"Really, Sybil—" Sir Oswald was beginning, a note of anger in his voice that certainly Sybil had never heard before.

He was interrupted. There was a sound of a car in the drive behind them. Maisie sprang back with a cry of welcome.

"Oh, Barbara! Barbara dear! Daddy, it is Barbara, come to see us at last."

Meanwhile Elizabeth, walking quickly, had gained the house. She delivered her message to Lady Davenant, and then went to her own room. Never the most Job-like of individuals, Sybil Lorrimer's remarks, coming after a morning of small irritations, had had the effect of raising her temper to boiling point. Her cheeks were hot, her eyes were flashing; it was the old Elizabeth who looked back at her out of the glass. She waited a minute or two to control herself, then, as she readjusted her hat she said half-aloud, "Oh, why can't she let me alone? If she knew how little I want to interfere with her plans—that I only want to be left in peace."

As she went downstairs she heard voices and recognized that there were visitors with Sir Oswald. Of course Maisie would be there too. She was sure of that, and she hesitated, frowning a little. Of all things she hated meeting strangers, yet Sir Oswald might expect her to look after the child.

As she stood there a voice said quickly, "No, don't you bother, Davenant, old man. I will find it myself. First floor, second room on left, you said, didn't you?"

Commonplace words enough, yet the very sound of them was enough to drive the blood from Elizabeth's cheeks, to make her catch at the balustrade for support as though her very limbs were paralysed. She cast one horrified glance around, then she turned quickly, her one thought for flight, she must at all hazards get away and hide herself from the gaze of the man below.

Her very haste brought about the catastrophe she was most anxious to avoid. The long end of her scarf caught in the carved edge of the balustrade. She tugged at it; the man, leaping upstairs two at a time behind her, paused, seeing she was in difficulties, and moved to help her. As he bent forward she gave one desperate wrench, there was a tearing sound, and she was free.

"Oh, I wish you had let me help you," the man said regretfully. "I am sure I would have done it without that—"

He stopped suddenly, the words on his lips dying away in horrified amazement.

For as Elizabeth bent forward her glasses had slipped down. He had looked right into her eyes.

"You!" he breathed, his voice dropping to a hoarse whisper. "You! What are you doing here?"

The governess thrust back her glasses, her breath coming in long painful gasps.

"I am Maisie's governess. Let me go, Mr. Carlyn."

Frank Carlyn fell back a step. "You are Maisie's governess! Good heavens!"

But the governess was hurrying away from him upstairs. Below in the hall Sir Oswald was waiting. Sybil Lorrimer and Barbara Burford stood in the doorway talking to Maisie. He sprang after that tall, dark figure already gaining the shelter of the corridor.

"This won't do," he said eagerly. "Don't you know that I have been searching everywhere for you?"

"I know that you will drive me from my poor little refuge," Elizabeth answered him bitterly. "Listen, Sir Oswald is calling you. Indeed I cannot talk to you now."

"Another time, then," Frank Carlyn pleaded. "We are dining here to-morrow. Will you be in the garden by the fountain afterwards?"

"If—if I can." Elizabeth caught the echo of Sybil Lorrimer's voice coming upstairs with Barbara. She burst away desperately. "But go—go now. Do you want to ruin me?" she gasped.

Chapter Seven

THE MOON was shining brightly—too brightly, Elizabeth Martin thought, shivering as she stood just inside the open library window. Dinner was practically over, she had heard Lady Davenant and her guests go into the drawing-room, but she could catch the sound of voices, the odour of tobacco smoke from the dining-room. She knew, however, that Sir Oswald never sat long over the wine, it was time she made her way to the summer-house near the fountain if she meant to keep her appointment with Frank Carlyn.

She let herself out quietly and stole across the lawn, taking care to keep within the shadow of the trees. Opposite the house there was the wall overlooking the Dutch garden, with a flight of steps leading down. Elizabeth glanced round fearfully as she hurried on, and started nervously as some nocturnal bird rustled among the trees. She ran across the garden. In the moonlight it was possible to see the softened radiance of the flowers gleaming like jewels in their quaint, stiff beds. At the farther side stood the summer-house; it was a favourite resort with the Davenants and their guests, combining as it did with a view of the Priory a glimpse of the distant Welsh hills.

Elizabeth drew a deep sigh of relief as she reached it, then she loosened the lace shawl in which she had shrouded her head and shoulders. As usual, she wore her smoke-coloured spectacles, and her hair was drawn low over her forehead, but even in the moonlight it was easy to see that her face was white, and that she was trembling all over.

She had not long to wait. Very soon she saw a dark form strolling across the lawn, and in another moment Frank Carlyn stood in the doorway.

Elizabeth moved forward.

"Well, I am here," she said quietly.

Carlyn started. "I ought to have been here first, but I couldn't get away before," he said apologetically, "I hope you have not been waiting long."

The words were commonplace enough, but the man's face was tense and strained, his hands were clenched nervously.

"Oh, what does that matter?" Elizabeth broke in impatiently. "The question is what do you want from me? Why did you bring me here at all? That is all that matters now."

"All that matters," Carlyn echoed hoarsely. "It seems to me that everything matters. Can't you see that something must be done—that things can't go on like this?"

Elizabeth put up her hands and threw back her shawl with a quick, impatient gesture as if it were stifling her. Then she moved a step nearer.

"What does that mean exactly? What things can't go on like this?"

Carlyn looked at her for a moment, his eyes resting on the sleek dark head, then his face hardened.

"You cannot stay here as Maisie's governess," he said abruptly.

Elizabeth did not move, not a muscle in her face stirred.

"Why not? Am I not in every way satisfactory? Has not Lady Davenant told you what a jewel of a governess she has secured? One with the highest references from her friend, Mrs. Sunningdale?" There was an indescribable bitterness in her tone.

Frank Carlyn's boyish face was downcast, his eyes sank before those of the woman opposite.

"Of course I have heard it," he burst out. "It seems to me that I have heard nothing else since I came here, but don't you see that all this makes it impossible for you to stop here?"

"All what?" There was no meekness in the governess's attitude now, her tone was both passionate and imperious.

Young Carlyn groaned aloud.

"You must know—you must understand that I can't keep silence when I know—the Davenants are Barbara's friends—"

"I think I do understand now," Elizabeth spoke in a dangerously quiet tone; she took off her glasses and threw them on the little rustic table beside her. "I am not good enough to be governess to Miss Burford's friend; but you—you are good enough to marry Miss Burford."

The scorn in her tone made the man wince as though he had been lashed.

There was a momentary silence, Elizabeth watching his changes of expression contemptuously. At last he spoke, and his tone was curiously changed:

"Heaven knows I don't want to minimize my share in the matter. If the worst had happened I should have spoken out, I should have—"

"You would have been very brave, doubtless," Elizabeth interrupted him mercilessly. "But, as matters stood, you choose the easier path. I congratulate you on your wisdom, Mr. Carlyn."

Frank Carlyn passed his hand over his forehead. He thought wearily that never before had man been placed in so horrible a dilemma. He had thought, as they drove to the Priory, that his duty was clear here, there could be no doubt about it. But here, looking at the woman's white face, at her blazing eyes, it seemed quite a different matter.

"I don't know what I ought to do," he capitulated weakly. "But I am sure, Mrs.—"

"Hush!" Elizabeth interrupted him sharply. "Not that. Never that name again. Remember that even the trees and bushes have ears sometimes. I will tell you what you must do, Mr.

Carlyn. You must go your way and leave me to go mine. Believe me, I shall not hurt the Davenants, or Maisie, and you—you can marry Miss Burford and forget all about me."

"That is so likely, is it not?" young Carlyn questioned moodily. "You don't know how the thought of that past day has haunted me ever since." He kicked a loose stone about carelessly, apparently watching that and not Elizabeth. "I couldn't imagine how you had got away. I thought—feared that some evil had befallen you."

"That I was dead, you mean?" Elizabeth said bitterly. "No, I was not so happy. I got out at the next station and by walking across country got on to another line, then I reached a friend and was safe. It isn't so difficult to escape the police as you think, Mr. Carlyn. And I couldn't stay to face things out. There were people"—she put up her hands to her throat as if the simple collar were about to choke her—"living then that it would have killed—"

"You couldn't have been blamed," Frank Carlyn began hotly.

"No?" Elizabeth laughed bitterly. "Yet I am not good enough to teach little Maisie. You are not very logical, Mr. Carlyn."

The man's face altered indefinably. "That seems quite different," he muttered sullenly. "And Davenant is such a good chap."

Elizabeth drew her shrouding cloak closely round her once more.

"Oh, yes, I quite appreciate your point of view," she said with a hard laugh. "But I shall not act upon it. I shall stay here until I am driven out. That is all there is to be said between us. For the future we are strangers."

"Oh, but—" Frank Carlyn protested weakly. "I shall want always to know where you are. And if you are in any difficulty you know I owe you—"

Elizabeth's slight figure stiffened. "Please do not go on. There are some things best left unsaid. Be assured that I, at any rate, am in no danger of forgetting what I owe to you."

She drew her shawl closely over head and shoulders and made a movement to pass him.

"One moment." He stepped before her quickly and then for the first time she saw that he held a small packet.

"This is yours. I have kept it ever since—that day, hoping that sometime I might have the opportunity of restoring it to you."

Elizabeth took it from him rather gingerly. "What is it? I don't know." Then, as she opened it and saw the three miniatures inside her expression changed. "My father's and mother's portraits. Oh, how did you get them?"

Neither of them heard a faint rustling among the trees behind the summer-house, no instinct warned them that they had an unseen auditor.

"I brought them away that day," Carlyn answered. "I knew that they might have led to your identification."

"I see." Elizabeth's tone was perceptibly altered. "Yes, I have wondered sometimes that they did not," she added. "Well, Mr. Carlyn, I could forgive you a great deal for bringing me these."

She slipped them inside her frock and with a slight inclination of her head moved away. Frank Carlyn followed her.

"But when shall I see you again? How shall I know where you are and what you are doing?"

A sarcastic smile played about Elizabeth's mouth.

"Is there any necessity that you should do either?" she questioned. "You seem to forget what lies between us, Mr. Carlyn. Best for you and best for me that we never hear one another's name again."

She walked quickly away from him, carefully keeping in the shadows that skirted the house.

Carlyn waited for a minute or two. He lighted a cigar and the end made a tiny, tapering light against the darkness of the trees. But presently he, too, went back to the house, walking openly across the lawn. When he had stepped inside the French window of the small drawing-room a third figure crept out from the bushes near the summer-house, a slight figure this and one that kept more carefully out of sight than even the governess had done.

Meanwhile, as Elizabeth was crossing the hall, she heard her name called in Sir Oswald's voice. He was just coming out of the library.

"Could you spare me a few minutes, Miss Martin? Three letters have come for me by the last post. I should be much obliged if you would read them to me."

"Certainly, Sir Oswald." The governess was breathing more heavily than usual, otherwise she betrayed no sign of the exciting interview through which she had just passed.

She followed Sir Oswald into the study, and opened the letters. There was nothing in them of importance, but she made brief notes of the answers he wished sent. Then she rose.

"If that is all, Sir Oswald, I will write the replies in the schoolroom."

"Thank you. And I suppose I must return to my guests, though a blind host is not sufficiently useful to be much missed. Why wouldn't you dine with us to-night, Miss Martin?"

The sudden question took the governess aback.

"I—Lady Davenant was kind enough to ask me," she stammered. "But I had a headache."

"Not bad enough to have prevented your dining, if you had wished, I fancy," Sir Oswald said shrewdly. "Do you know that I have promised to read you a lesson on unsociability, Miss Martin? Lady Treadstone—"

"Ah!" Elizabeth caught her breath sharply.

"Lady Treadstone tells me you have refused every invitation she has sent you," Sir Oswald pursued. He was looking faintly amused in spite of the apparent sternness of his tone. "What excuse can you make for yourself?"

"None!" Elizabeth, answered him sharply. I do not wish to visit Lady Treadstone, Sir Oswald."

Sir Oswald raised his brows. "Are you not a little unsociable, Miss Martin? Lady Treadstone has taken a great fancy to you, she told me as much. Even if it should not be reciprocal—"

"It is not!" Elizabeth interrupted him, holding up her head with a little proud gesture that had once been habitual with her. "I do not like Lady Treadstone"—her hand straying to the front of her bodice, clutching at the miniature case—"I—I hate her."

"You hate her?" Sir Oswald was frankly amazed. Pleasant, kindly Lady Treadstone seemed to him the last person in the world to have inspired the depth of dislike of which the girl's tone spoke. "But you know so little of her. Don't you think you—"

"I know quite enough of her." Elizabeth's tone was hard and resentful. To herself she was saying that it was cruel that all the mistakes in her past should meet her here, that never should she be able to live it down. "I beg your pardon, Sir Oswald. If you wish me to take Maisie to lunch with her, of course it is a different matter, but for myself I do not wish to visit or even to see Lady Treadstone."

Sir Oswald bent his head. Blind as he was, he could not help realizing that there was some hint of mystery here, but he was of too loyal a nature to question her.

"As you like," he said simply. "I certainly should not wish you to do anything you disliked. You believe that, I hope." He moved forward a step as he spoke and held out his hand. Some forlorn note in Elizabeth's voice had roused the instinct of protection that is dormant in every man.

He did not understand that tone and gesture alike were a revelation to Elizabeth, the betrayal of a feeling whose very existence she had never suspected and from which she shrank as far from some deadly peril. A rush of crimson swept over her face, then receded, leaving it deadly white. She ignored the outstretched hand.

"You are exceedingly kind, Sir Oswald," she managed to say as she opened the door. "I hope I shall never forget the gratitude I owe both to you and Lady Davenant."

Chapter Eight

"YOU ARE quite sure you don't mind my having the car, Oswald?" Sybil Lorrimer looked in at the library door.

Sir Oswald was sitting near the window. He raised his head.

"Why, of course I don't. I shall be only too delighted," he said, speaking with more truth than Sybil guessed. That she had asked to have the car for a long day's shopping in Birmingham meant that they would have a day without her at the Priory. And a day without Sybil was beginning to be a day of peace for Sir Oswald. The gratitude and mild liking he had formerly entertained for her was rapidly turning into something very like absolute dislike. It seemed to him that she was becoming ubiquitous, he found it impossible to stir out of doors without meeting her, and in the house she was always at his elbow with offers of service.

More than once Sir Oswald had tried to hint to his mother that Sybil's stay had lasted long enough, but Lady Davenant liked the girl. In some way she had made herself necessary to her, and, noting her unwillingness, Sir Oswald had ceased to press the matter.

To-day he had been sitting quietly in his chair, thinking of Elizabeth: of her sweet, low tones, of the faint, elusive fragrance that clung about her. He was asking himself what could be the cause of the coldness with which she was undoubtedly treating him; it was impossible that he could have offended her, and yet the difference was unmistakable.

With a sigh of annoyance he heard Sybil come farther into the room. He wished he had gone into his study where he was less likely to be invaded.

But Sybil was apparently not in one of her talkative moods. He heard her cross the room, then there followed a rustling of paper. He bore it in silence for a minute of two, then he said in a tone of mild exasperation:

"What are you doing, Sybil? Surely you have the papers in the morning-room?"

"Not the paper I want," Sybil answered. "You only have one copy and it is brought here. I have found what I wanted now. It was only an advertisement I saw the other day."

"Of a new hat shop?" Sir Oswald questioned jestingly.

"No, not that," Sybil answered absently. She was copying an address into her notebook. It stood at the bottom of a paragraph which at first sight it seemed impossible to connect with pretty, dainty Sybil Lorrimer.

"Private Detective Agency," it was headed. "Messrs. Gregg and Stubbs are prepared to conduct inquiries on the newest lines. Delicate investigations arranged with the utmost secrecy. Highest testimonials can be given. Address: Messrs. Gregg and Stubbs, 2A, Palmer Buildings, New Fish Street, Birmingham."

Sybil closed her notebook and put it in her satchel. Then she hesitated a moment.

"Oswald, I—"

There were voices outside. Maisie and her governess were coming downstairs. Sir Oswald rose as quickly as he could.

"I must speak to Miss Martin. Excuse me, Sybil."

Sybil's fair face hardened, her momentary irresolution vanished.

"Well, good-bye then," she called out with assumed gaiety as she ran down the steps and got into the aiting car.

The great Metropolis of the Midlands was about an hour's drive from the Priory. The road for the most part lay through pleasant, wooded country, sparsely populated until they reached the suburbs of the town.

Sybil did not tell the chauffeur to drive to New Fish Street. Instead she got out in New Street and directed the man to drive to and wait for her at the nearest garage. She had her own reasons for wishing her visit to Messrs. Gregg and Stubbs to remain unknown.

Even when she had got rid of the car she did not hurry herself; she strolled in and out of two or three shops, making trifling purchases, though it was easy to see that her thoughts were elsewhere.

But at last she made up her mind to face the real business of the day. New Fish Street was some little distance away, in the new part of the town, but Sybil found her way there with but little difficulty. Palmer Buildings was a conspicuous block near the end of the street; it was apparently let out as offices, and Messrs. Gregg and Stubbs occupied the second floor.

Sybil stopped a moment and glanced round nervously before entering the centre passage—but, no—there was certainly no one who would know her among the busy throng in the street. It seemed to her that even the lift-boy looked at her curiously as she gave the address of Messrs. Gregg and Stubbs. More than once she felt inclined to give up her expedition and turn back, but she was a little reassured by the businesslike aspect of the offices that confronted her.

Mr. Gregg was in and would be at liberty in a few minutes, she learned on application to a solemn-looking youth in spectacles, who to her relief seemed to take no interest in her whatever. He showed her into a small waiting-room and retired.

Sybil had time to ascertain that certain small trophies of hers were safe in her bag, and also to arrange in what words to open her business, before he returned to conduct her to Mr. Gregg.

Sybil looked about her curiously as she entered. Mr. Gregg rose when the door opened and placed a large leather chair for her, with its face to the light.

He was a tall, spare-looking man, with a stoop that seemed habitual about his thin shoulders; and, for the rest, he was clean-shaven with mild-looking blue eyes that seemed to be perpetually blinking. Sybil though he looked more like a professor or a student than a private detective.

He had resumed his seat at his writing-table.

"You wished to see me?" he said interrogatively.

"Yes." Sybil fumbled with her satchel. It was more difficult to begin than she had anticipated. "You—you inquire into other people's pasts, don't you?" she said abruptly.

Mr. Gregg bowed. "If anybody has reason for us to do so, madam."

He was a little puzzled by Sybil. She was not married, so there was no peccant husband to be inquired about. It must be a lover, he decided, but women of Sybil's class did not often come to him for help. His interest was distinctly roused.

"And you don't let them know that they are being inquired about, or anyone else?" Sybil went on feverishly. "So, if it all comes to nothing, there is no harm done?"

"No harm at all," the detective acquiesced. "I think we know our work, madam, and secrecy is one of the first essentials. You may safely trust yourself in our hands."

"Yes, I thought so," Sybil said in a relieved tone. "I want you to find out all you can about the past of a woman who is a governess at Davenant Priory to my little cousin, Sir Oswald Davenant's daughter."

A shade of surprise flitted over Mr. Gregg's face. This was not at all what he had expected to hear.

"Certainly, madam."

He drew a heavy ledger towards him and turned over the leaves. Then with his pen uplifted he waited, looking at Sybil.

"Will you give me any particulars you can of the lady—any reason you may have for thinking her past may hold some secret? I presume you had references with her?"

"My aunt had," Sybil corrected. "Written ones only from a great friend, Mrs. Sunningdale, who is now in India. She was most enthusiastic about Miss Martin, I believe."

Mr. Gregg blinked at her. "I presume you have some definite reason for being dissatisfied with Miss Martin, for making inquiries about her?"

"I am dissatisfied with her in every way," Sybil said with gathering energy. "I am convinced that she is an adventuress, but I want you to find me some definite grounds on which to proceed."

Mr. Gregg's blue eyes still blinked. All this was very interesting from his point of view, but he saw clearly enough that the affair might resolve itself into merely a matter of jealousy between two women and he felt by no means certain of Sybil Lorrimer's ability to pay his expenses. Messrs. Gregg and Stubbs were not inclined to work for nothing.

"But, Miss Lorrimer," he said, with a slight hesitation in his manner, "you may be quite right, very possibly you are, but I must say again, I suppose you have some reason for your suspicion, for speaking of Miss Martin as an adventuress?"

The interview was not proceeding precisely as Sybil had expected. Questioned thus, her distrust of the governess seemed almost baseless. Still, some instinct stronger than reason told her that she was on the right track, that there was some secret in Miss Martin's past, and she was determined to discover it.

"It isn't easy to put the reason for one's suspicions into words," she said slowly. "Of course if it were more than suspicion I should have no need to come to you, Mr. Gregg."

A movement of the detective's eyelids showed that he appreciated this thrust. He began to see that this fluffy, golden-haired lady had more in her than he had imagined.

"Her very appearance suggests a disguise," Sybil went on. "She has large grey eyes, apparently quite strong, and yet she constantly wears smoke-coloured glasses, and however hot the weather is I have never seen her out of doors even in the park except with her hat and her face swathed in a veil. She gives neuralgia as the reason, but she evidently dislikes speaking about it."

"Um-m." Mr. Gregg was making some entries in his ledger. "Will you describe the lady, madam."

"She is tall," Sybil began, "tall, with good features and a very fair complexion and masses of black hair—too black, and not shingled. I am sure it is dyed."

Mr. Gregg permitted himself a smile. "That is not so very unusual, madam, I fancy. Everybody does not admire shingling, either. What age is she?"

"I should say under thirty," Sybil said vaguely. "What with her veil and her glasses it is difficult to see enough of her to be sure."

Mr. Gregg tapped restlessly on the open page of his ledger.

"Well, madam, I think it would be well to consider what you are doing before we go on with the matter. It is sure to be expensive—such inquiries always are—and I am bound to tell you that you seem to have but the slightest of grounds for your suspicion of this lady."

Sybil's small face looked obstinate. "I intend to go on," she said quietly. "But of course, Mr. Gregg—" She stopped suddenly and opened her bag. "I was forgetting. But I don't know that you will consider these of any importance. I came across them by accident in Miss Martin's room, among some things she was burning." She held out the photograph and the tiny curl of red gold hair.

Mr. Gregg looked a little bored as he took them in his hand, then his expression changed indefinably; he bent over them and studied them intently. At last he glanced up.

"You are sure these belong to Miss Martin?"

"Quite sure," Sybil returned laconically.

Mr. Gregg swept them both into an envelope.

"Well, Miss Lorrimer, we will do the best we can for you and as soon as we learn anything definite we will communicate with you."

"One more thing I might mention," Sybil said as she stood up. "Miss Martin, though they met as strangers, is evidently on most familiar terms with a man who dined at the Priory last week, a Mr. Carlyn, of Carlyn Hall. I feel sure he knows the secret of her past."

"Mr. Carlyn. Ah!" The detective said no more as he opened the door for her. He was apparently lost in a brown study.

Sybil opened her bag again. "I believe it is usual to pay something on account." She laid a twenty-pound note on the table.

Mr. Gregg pushed it back to her, blinking benevolently.

"No, no! My dear madam, wait till we have done something."

He saw her out with grave politeness, then he went back to his office and took up his speaking-tube.

"Send Mr. Marlowe to me at once."

There was an air of repressed excitement about him as he waited the coming of the ex-constable from Carlyn.

The ex-policeman looked much as usual, save that out of uniform he seemed a trifle less portly and important. He looked at Mr. Gregg in some surprise.

"You sent for me, sir?"

"Yes," Mr. Gregg replied, taking the photograph from its envelope and handing it to him. "Sit down, Marlowe. Can you tell me anything about this?"

Marlowe glanced at it leisurely and then he gave a cry of amazement.

"Why, if it isn't a photo of John Winter, who was murdered in the Home Wood at Carlyn Hall a year last spring. Where did you get it, sir?"

Mr. Gregg rubbed his hands together.

"Ah! 'Thereby hangs a tale.' But I thought I wasn't mistaken. You will have to prepare for special work for the next few days, Marlowe."

Chapter Nine

"AND YOU will tell me a story, Barbara, and you will come to tea in the schoolroom with me and Miss Martin?" cried Maisie, dancing round the girl in her excitement.

"If Miss Martin will ask me," smiled Barbara.

On the conclusion of her stay with her other friends in the neighbourhood Barbara had come to pay a long-promised visit to the Davenants. Not Frank Carlyn. The day after the dinner-party at the Priory he had been summoned home on urgent business, much to Elizabeth's relief.

All the Davenants liked Barbara, who had been a friend of Sir Oswald's poor young wife, while with Maisie she was a special favourite. She had seen the governess a few minutes before breakfast. Miss Martin had made but little impression upon her beyond striking her as a silent and not very agreeable young person.

Now Elizabeth was standing just inside the open door of the schoolroom waiting for Maisie. Above all things she was anxious to see as little as possible of Frank Carlyn's fiancée. It was easy to pretend not to hear Barbara's courteous reference to her with regard to the projected tea-party in the midst of Maisie's chatter, but it would be difficult to avoid the offered visit, and Elizabeth was afraid of Miss Burford, and of what she might find out.

Maisie was doing her best to pull Barbara into the room with her.

"Come and see my French exercise. There are only two mistakes, so daddy is going to give me a box of bon-bons."

Barbara yielded. "Ah, well! I think I really can't resist that."

"I'm afraid Maisie is a little tiresome," Miss Martin said apologetically. She was standing near the window and the morning sunlight was streaming full upon her; in its clear radiance her hair looked oddly black. Barbara's puzzled gaze rested upon it. It seemed so strange that so young a woman should dye her hair, and yet Barbara asked herself, looking at it, could there be any doubt? The governess flushed under her scrutiny, and in a moment Barbara looked away. Miss Martin's pallor seemed to have transferred itself to her now, and she said little as she glanced at Maisie's vaunted exercise.

A servant appeared in the doorway.

"Sir Oswald would be glad if you could spare him a few minutes, miss," he said, addressing himself to the governess. "It is an important letter that needs answering. Miss Maisie is to go to her ladyship."

"I will come at once," Miss Martin said, moving to the door with an unmistakable air of relief. "Come, Maisie!"

"I will take Maisie to Lady Davenant," Barbara promised, and the governess hurried off.

As she went down the passage she heard Maisie coaxing, "You will come to the schoolroom tea to-day, Barbara?" And she caught the girl's clear-toned reply, "I will tell you the story, Maisie, dear, but I don't know about the tea. If I ask Granny to give it us in the boudoir, won't that do as well?"

Elizabeth went on to the study. Sir Oswald had come back from town the preceding day. The verdict of the specialist had not been quite so favourable as the local doctor had hoped. The eyes were better, decidedly better, he said, but there must be an interval of three months before the operation which would give Sir Oswald back his sight could be attempted.

Three months seemed but a little time to wait to the rest of the world, but to Sir Oswald, who had been confidently reckoning on his immediate restoration to sight, it was an eternity.

He was looking dull and depressed when Elizabeth went in, and gave her only the briefest of directions as to the reply when she read his letter to him. But when she rose he stopped her.

"You have heard my sentence, Miss Martin? Three months more of this horrible darkness and helplessness?"

"Yes, I have heard," the aloofness there had been in Elizabeth's voice of late had gone; it was very pitiful now.

"Why don't you tell me to be thankful it is no worse?" Sir Oswald questioned with a reckless laugh. "That is the stock remark. Good heavens! Three months more of this total blindness! I wonder whether you know—whether anybody knows—what it means to me."

"One can only think of the getting well in the end," Elizabeth said gently.

Sir Oswald shrugged his shoulders "How do I know the fellow may not say the same thing at the end of this three months? But I must not weary you, Miss Martin. You don't know how much your tact and sympathy have helped me since you came to the Priory."

"I am very glad that I have been able to be of use to you, Sir Oswald," Elizabeth said quietly.

Sir Oswald felt that she was turning away. He got up, moving towards her uncertainly, all his prudent resolutions swept to the winds by his longing to have her sympathy, to keep her presence with him.

"Miss Martin—Elizabeth," he said hoarsely. "I shall want your help more than ever now, won't you give it to me?"

He could hear her quickened breathing. He knew that she was struggling to retain her self-control.

"I shall always be glad to do anything I can, Sir Oswald," she murmured.

He stepped forward quickly, her agitation teaching him coolness, he caught one of her slim, soft hands in his.

"That is not all I want, Elizabeth; I want you, dear—to be with me always—to be my wife."

The governess struggled to free her hand.

"Oh, this is madness, Sir Oswald!" she cried.

"Let me go, please."

But Sir Oswald's clasp only tightened on the fluttering fingers.

"Why should it be madness, Elizabeth? Is it impossible that you should care for a blind man?"

"Oh, no—not that!" Elizabeth cried quickly, and Sir Oswald's face brightened.

"What is it, then?" he questioned. "I have learned in my blindness and helplessness to care for you very dearly, Elizabeth. Don't tell me that it is hopeless. Let me teach you."

"No, no, no!" Elizabeth's voice caught in her throat in a muffled shriek. "Sir Oswald, I tell you again you are mad—mad! You are asking a woman to marry you of whom you know nothing, whom you have never even seen."

Sir Oswald still held her hand, but some of the passion died out of his face.

"I know you, Elizabeth—that is enough for me. I think I fell in love with you the first time you came into the room with your sweet voice, your gentle, tender ways. And if I haven't seen you—well, I made Perkins read aloud Mrs. Sunningdale's description of you one day. I think I have got it by heart. But I should have known what you looked like without that, my dear; I couldn't help it, I think."

Elizabeth stood still, her fingers lying inert in his clasp.

"What do you mean by Mrs. Sunningdale's description of me? I don't understand," she questioned hoarsely.

A faint smile crept under Sir Oswald's brown moustache. "I heard my mother telling Sybil the other day she had lost the first letter Mrs. Sunningdale wrote about you, and I laughed to myself. That letter is calmly reposing in one of the drawers of my writing-table. It was brought to me to hear what Mrs. Sunningdale said about Maisie's new governess, and I shall not part with it until I see the original Elizabeth."

"What did she say?" Elizabeth asked abruptly. There was still that curious immobility in her attitude.

Sir Oswald's smile deepened.

"I wonder if you will tell me again that I am mad, Elizabeth, when you know that I can repeat her description word for word? Listen! 'Miss Martin is above middle height, slight and dark, with one of the most lovable faces I have ever seen; she has masses of dark brown hair and pretty, kind brown eyes.' So you see, Miss Martin, I have some idea what you are like. I have pictured you very often in my thoughts, the clouds of hair shadowing the most lovable little face in the world, the pretty, kind, brown eyes."

The woman with the grey eyes and black hair, listening, tore her hands from his with a moan. So near—so near she had been, nay, she was—to detection. And she had thought herself so safe from all the world but Frank Carlyn.

"And now I want those same kind brown eyes to come and be eyes for me," Sir Oswald went on. "Elizabeth, you will take pity on me?"

"No, no!" The grey eyes were full of wild terror now. "I can't! Indeed I can't!"

It was impossible for Sir Oswald to mistake either the finality or the pain in her tone, his face grew suddenly graver, sterner.

"Do you mean that there is some real obstacle?" he asked slowly.

"Yes—a barrier that can never be passed. I can never marry. I shall never think of marrying." Elizabeth's sobs were rising now in her throat, threatening to choke her.

Sir Oswald, in his blindness, felt very far away.

"I can't understand," he said helplessly. "Does this mean that you care for someone else—that you are engaged—married even?"

"No," Elizabeth said faintly. She was telling him the bare truth, and yet when she heard his sigh she felt that it was worse than the cruellest of lies.

"But you have cared for someone else?" Sir Oswald hazarded.

"Ah, no, no!" Elizabeth cried, putting up her hands to her throat.

"Then," said Sir Oswald slowly, "if you are not bound to anyone, if you don't care, if you never have cared for anyone, I shall not give up hope."

"Oh, you will! You must!" Elizabeth's breath came quick and fast, she fought despairingly to regain her self-control, not to yield to the impulse that bade her thrust herself and her story on Sir Oswald Davenant's mercy. "Don't you see that unless you promise to forget—to give up—I can't stay here—at the Priory?" she said, with a hoarse catch in her throat. "And I have nowhere else to go. I am so lonely."

As he heard the last words Sir Oswald's face softened and grew very pitiful. He moved a little nearer with his uncertain, stumbling steps, but Elizabeth would not trust herself within touch of those strong, kind hands again.

"I am at your mercy, Elizabeth," he said gravely. "You may rely at least upon it that I will not speak of it again while you are in my house unless you yourself give me permission. On your part—"

He paused and Elizabeth watched his face anxiously. He went on in a minute. "You must promise to stay here and be good to Maisie and me as you have been hitherto. We can't do without you, either of us, Elizabeth."

The hint of weakness in the strong man's voice touched the governess as no pleading could have done. For one instant she stood beside him, warm, palpitating, hesitating, the next she had caught sight of herself in a small Venetian mirror inlet into the wall opposite her, and hurried breathlessly from the room.

She ran upstairs. On the lawn beneath she could hear Maisie chattering to Barbara Burford. She would go down in a minute or two, but she must have breathing space to think matters over first. That Sir. Oswald should propose to her, want to marry her, had never entered her calculations, changed though his manner had been of late. She had always heard that some men looked upon a flirtation with a governess as a recognized form of amusement, and she supposed that her lot was to be the same as others. But now everything was altered; apart from the fact that she stood on the verge of detection she knew that what had passed would render it impossible for her to remain at the Priory long; and, as she had told Sir Oswald, she had nowhere else to go. Tears welled up in her eyes as she glanced round the pretty bedroom she had learned to look upon as her own.

There was a knock at her door. Eliza, the schoolroom maid, stood in the doorway, her pretty childish face showing unmistakable signs of tears.

"What is it, Eliza?" asked Elizabeth kindly. She liked the girl, who had waited on her since her coming to the Priory, but just at present she found her own worries all-absorbing.

"My mother is ill," the girl said tearfully. "Her ladyship says I can go home at once, and Ellen can wait on you, but I thought that I should like to tell you myself—" She paused expectantly.

For once Elizabeth's ready sympathy failed her.

"Your mother is ill, Eliza?" she repeated dully. "I—I am very sorry."

Chapter Ten

"WHERE ARE you going?" Maisie popped her head through the banisters just as Barbara, ready equipped for walking, came into the hall.

The girl looked up and smiled. "Oh, just for a walk," she said vaguely.

"Miss Martin and I are going to take some soup to Mrs. Archer at the south lodge. You wouldn't like to come with us?" Maisie said persuasively.

"Not to-day, I think—" Barbara said slowly.

Maisie stamped her foot.

"It never is to-day," she said with childish vehemence. "And I thought you would come and have tea with us in the schoolroom and be ever so nice, not stuck up like Sybil. And now I really believe you are worse. I am disappointed in you, Barbara."

"Are you really?" Barbara laughed in spite of herself. "I am sorry it is as bad as that, Maisie. But of course I will have tea with you this afternoon if Miss Martin will ask me when I come back. But I can't walk down to the lodge. I have a big thing that I must do by myself."

"Like daddy does?" Maisie said wisely. "Oh, well, if you will come to tea, Barbara, I will forgive you. You really are a dear." She sprang down the stairs two steps at a time, and bestowed an enthusiastic kiss on the girl.

Barbara laughed again as she returned it, but her face wore a very worried expression as she closed the front door behind her and set off across the park. Life was becoming a very complex thing now to Barbara Burford. Everything had seemed to lie so straight before her until she came to the Priory, and then a few minutes had sufficed to change everything. She was staying much longer than she intended at the Davenants'. She had caught eagerly at Lady Davenant's invitation to extend her visit, thinking to give herself breathing space and perhaps to find out that she was troubling herself needlessly. But now her father had written to recall her, she was wanted at home and in the parish, one week longer was all that he was willing to allow her. And Barbara was faced by the fact that she must make up her mind on a very important matter before her return.

All her life, as it seemed to her, she had loved Frank Carlyn. For years their friendship had been an established thing, no one had doubted that it would ultimately end as it had. There had been a few months last year when a sort of estrangement had grown up between them, but it had been ended by Frank's proposal and since then Barbara had been happier than she had ever been in all her life. Happier—and more miserable. For now Barbara was deliberating with herself whether it was not her duty to put an end to the engagement. Did Frank Carlyn care for her, as he could care for someone else—nay, as he had cared and perhaps did care for someone else? Barbara could not answer this question to her satisfaction. All this time of her engagement she had been haunted by the feeling that, old friends as they were, something stood always between her and Frank, some figure or shadow of the past. Now it was assuming a more tangible shape, and Barbara was faced by a problem more difficult than anything her young, unguarded life had hitherto encountered.

No solution had occurred to her as she entered the mossy wood, and turned slowly down the path.

She knit her brows as she walked on deep in thought. So absorbed was she that but for a chance movement on the part of a man lounging against a tree trunk at the side of the road she would have passed him unobserved.

Then she looked up, and after a moment's bewilderment stopped short in surprise at sight of a familiar face.

"Why, Marlowe, is it you? What brings you to this part of the world?"

The ex-policeman touched his cap.

"My missus comes from these parts, miss. Her people have a bit of a farm over Cowley way, and she hasn't been just the thing lately, so I brought her over for a change. I'm only here for the week-end. I couldn't leave the business any longer. And how's all the people down at Carlyn, miss, if you will pardon me for asking, the rector and the young Squire—Mr. Carlyn?"

"They are quite well, thank you," Barbara answered mechanically.

She was recalling what she had heard when Constable Marlowe left Carlyn. He and his wife had come into money. It was said that he was giving up the police force on the strength of it and taking a small business somewhere in the Black Country. It seemed plausible, and yet Barbara could not help feeling that something lay behind the story. The man was glib enough with his tale, but she fancied she had detected a shade of discomfiture in his face when she recognized him.

"I am sorry to hear Mrs. Marlowe has not been well," she went on after a pause. "Where are you living now—I forget?"

"Over in Burchell, a village on the other side of Stoke," Marlowe lied glibly. "My uncle left me a bit of a shop there, china and so forth, and we are making a decent living at it, and it doesn't take it out of a man like the police force."

"No, I daresay not," Barbara assented absently.

The man was obviously anxious to move on, and she had no excuse to detain him. He touched his hat and she nodded her good-bye. Yet as she pursued her walk she felt vaguely uneasy. Marlowe's presence in Castor might mean so much or so little.

Meanwhile Mr. Marlowe was cursing himself for a stupid fool. He had heard there was a young lady stopping at the Priory, but in his preoccupation with other matters he had failed to ask her name. This neglect had brought this recognition on himself, with the possible ruin of all plans. He had nearly reached the edge of the wood when he caught sight of the figure for which he had been waiting. It was a pleasant, rosy-faced young woman in black who approached him.

"Well, what luck?" he demanded impatiently.

"Give me a minute," she responded, pressing her hand to her side. "I am out of breath with climbing that hill. I have got the place."

"That is right," he said heartily, his face clearing. "When do you go in?"

The girl laughed. "To-night. I haven't let the grass grow under my feet, have I?"

Marlowe looked at her admiringly. "You are a good girl. I always did say you were smart, Susy."

Few people would have taken the two for brother and sister. Susan was as slim and alert as Marlowe was portly and phleg-matic looking. The girl, however, was devoted to her brother. She had as great a belief in his powers as he had himself, and it was mainly on her advice that he had thrown up his position in the police to work for Mr. Gregg. That gentleman had been one of the detectives sent down to Carlyn to investigate the death of John Winter. He had started a detective agency on his own account soon afterwards, and the opinion he had formed of Mr. Marlowe's abilities had led him to offer him a liberal salary to join him. This was not the first time that Susy had been called upon to help in their plans, and more than once she had been found invaluable.

Marlowe had soon discovered that his inquiry into the past of the governess at the Priory was hopeless from the outside. Nothing was known of her in the village, and unless on an errand for Lady Davenant she seldom went beyond the Park, and the woods close to the house, with her little charge.

The fact that the situation of schoolroom maid was vacant at the Priory gave him his opportunity. Susan was the very person to wait on Miss Martin and incidentally to find out all that that unfortunate young woman wished to remain hidden.

Sybil Lorrimer had professed a previous acquaintance with the girl, and acted as her reference, and Susan's obtaining the situation was a foregone conclusion. Nevertheless Marlowe had been afraid of some hitch and his relief was unmistakable.

"You saw Miss Lorrimer?" he questioned.

Susan nodded. "That is why I am a bit late. She took me up to her bedroom saying I was an old friend, and she did talk. How she hates Miss Martin!"

Marlowe looked thoughtful. "I know. But look here, Susan, my girl. I don't suppose my letter made it clear to you that Miss Lorrimer's interests and ours—Mr. Gregg's and mine—may not run just on the same lines. All that Miss Lorrimer wants is to get rid of the governess from the Priory."

Susan looked wise. "I gathered as much. Miss Martin stands in Miss Lorrimer's way with Sir Oswald. Of course she wants to marry him herself."

"Yes, that is her point of view," Marlowe assented. "But what we mean to find out is whether this Miss Martin isn't somebody who has been wanted by the police for over a year. If she is— why, there will be a big reward for the ones that find her. As for getting rid of her from the Priory, that is an easy matter, and we could do it to-morrow as easy as that," snapping his fingers. "But it doesn't suit our purpose. You must temporize with Miss Lorrimer, Susan, temporize—that is the word."

Susan's rosy face looked thoughtful, she wrinkled up her brows and pursed up her lips until a certain comical resemblance to her brother made itself apparent.

"Miss Lorrimer will not be a patient person to deal with, I can see that. But it ought not to take me long to find out what you want. Still, you remember that your letter wasn't very definite. You merely told me to go to the Priory and apply for the post of schoolroom maid, and that Miss Lorrimer would be my reference. Oh, yes, and that I was wanted to watch the governess. All the rest of the explanation I have had comes from Miss Lorrimer, and the chief ground she gave me to work on was that she was sure the governess dyed her hair. There is nothing very extraordinary in that."

The ex-constable's eyes looked cunning. "Ah! And yet there is more turns on that than Miss Lorrimer knows, or you think, Susy. For if she is the woman we want she is not tall and dark, but tall and fair, leastways with hair that some folks call auburn and some golden."

"Why, Jim!" Susy's eyes were growing rounder, the rosy colour in her cheeks deepened, her breath quickened. "Tall and auburn-haired," she repeated. "Jim, you don't never think that it is—"

"Sh! Don't say it," her brother interrupted her. "There are things that are best left unsaid, even when we are alone like this. You are a sharp one, Susy! I knew you would tumble to it, though I didn't think it would be as soon as this."

Susy had not recovered from her astonishment.

"Well, to think of it being that," she ejaculated. "The thing I have always wanted to be in. You may depend upon me doing my very best for that, Jim."

"I knew I could," her brother responded with a gratified look. "Well, now, you see what you have to do. You just find out if she is—this woman; and then we can manage Miss Lorrimer's business as well as our own. Search her boxes. You have your keys. There must be proof of identification somewhere."

"Must be," Susan nodded. "As for the hair, you leave that to me. I know a trick that will manage that. But there is one thing that puzzles me, if she is the person you are looking for, how did she get in as governess at the Priory?

"Ay! There is wheels within wheels. And that's one of the many nuts we have got to crack." her brother observed enigmatically. "Miss Martin was recommended to Lady Davenant by a great friend of hers, a Mrs. Sunningdale."

"Then I don't see how—" Susan said in a puzzled tone.

"That recommendation didn't do her much good, however," her brother pursued imperturbably. "Since a fortnight before this—lady—arrived at the Priory, the Miss Elizabeth Martin who was Mrs. Sunningdale's governess died of blood poisoning at a hospital in Camden Town."

Chapter Eleven

BARBARA sat in her own room writing a letter. To speak more accurately, she had apparently written a great many letters, and consigned them all in turn to the same receptacle—the waste-paper-basket. She took up a new sheet of paper and began again.

"My dear Frank."

Then she paused once more. How was she to say it? In what words should she tell Frank Carlyn that she could never be his wife? For Barbara's mind was made up at last. Frank should be free, it might be that he owed something to that other one, it might be that he had only proposed to her—Barbara—out of pique. At any rate she would not share a divided affection, and her proud, little head went up at the thought.

She turned back to her paper. After all, the shortest statement of fact would be sufficient—she would couch it in the baldest possible terms. Frank would not criticize it overmuch. Probably he would be glad to get his freedom, she said to herself bitterly.

"Don't you think we have made a mistake," she wrote. "We were friends, such good friends, but to think that we could be anything more was, as I say, a mistake. Therefore, Frank, I want you to set me free from our engagement, and remain my friend still." She hesitated a moment, how was she to end it? Then she wrote "Barbara," as steadily as ever, folded the paper, tucked it into its envelope and addressed it to "Frank Carlyn Esq., Carlyn Hall," as quickly as possible lest she should change her mind and this latest note should share the fate of its predecessors.

Then she sat back in her chair and tears gathered in her hazel eyes, as she thought of the two to whom she knew this decision of hers would mean the bitterest disappointment—her father and old Mrs. Carlyn. They, like their children, had been firm friends for more years than they cared to count, and Barbara knew that her marriage with Frank had been very dear to both their hearts. Still she told herself that what she had done was unavoidable—had been unavoidable from the first—if only she had had the courage to own it. For Frank she could see no way out of the tangle, but, if he did not know his own mind, it was plainly her duty to make the decision for him.

Nevertheless life looked a very dreary thing to Barbara, and the tears coursed down her cheeks as she contemplated it.

They were still wet when there was a knock at the door and Maisie's voice called reproachfully.

"I do believe you have forgotten your promise again, Barbara. You said you would come to tea this afternoon, and we have been waiting for you, and at last Miss Martin said I might come and fetch you."

Barbara hastily removed the traces of her tears, and opened the door.

"I didn't know it was so late, Maisie dear," she said apologetically. "But I hadn't forgotten. I'm so glad you came for me, dear."

Maisie caught her hand.

"Come on, then. But you look as if you had a headache"—eyeing her critically—"and Miss Martin has had one all day, so I am afraid it will not be a very lively tea-party after all."

Elizabeth was standing behind the tea-tray as Maisie threw open the schoolroom door and announced Miss Barbara Burford, imitating the butler's best style. It was evident that preparations had been made for a visitor, there was a choice assortment of cakes and three kinds of jam.

"Now Maisie will be happy," Miss Martin said with a smile. "It is very good of you to spare us the time, Miss Burford."

"Not at all, I am sure I shall enjoy it," Barbara responded politely, but her tone was cold in spite of her best efforts.

"This is where you are to sit," Maisie went on, pulling her to the side of the table. "And mind you say 'What a comfortable chair!' Our visitors always do. I am going to sit at the bottom of the table opposite Miss Martin. She is mistress and I am master, like Daddy. That is his place. What a feast they will have to give us when he can see again, won't they, Miss Martin?"

The governess smiled a little as she poured out the tea.

"I expect you will not let them forget that, Maisie."

"No, I shall not!" the child nodded. "Because I shall be so glad, so very glad, when my dear Daddy can see again. I wish every one could see like you and me, Barbara, and didn't have to wear glasses and things. I expect Miss Martin does too, don't you, Miss Martin? Because she has such pretty eyes really, and she looks so nice without her glasses." Barbara did not look at the woman sitting at the top of the table, she gazed straight before her through the open window, where already the long strands of Virginia creeper were turning to their autumn glories of crimson and golden brown.

"I expect most people look better without glasses," she said in an uninterested tone. "But, Maisie, haven't you been taught not to make personal remarks?"

"I don't think people mind if you say they look nice," Maisie urged shrewdly. "It is if you say they don't that they are cross. Now Miss Martin—"

"Has heard quite enough about herself," interrupted the subject of Maisie's comments truthfully. "Come Maisie, can't you find something more interesting to tell Miss Burford? Your cat—"

"Oh, yes. I thought I had something to tell you, Barbara; my cat has four kittens, two tabby, one black and one tortoise-shell. Isn't it extraordinary that they should be so varied?"

Miss Martin and Barbara exchanged a smile, as Maisie proceeded to recount the excellences of her pets. But by and by Barbara's attention wandered from the kitten's beauties to her own troubles. Her eyes strayed mechanically to the woman at the top of the table, and rested for a moment on the dark hair. Then her gaze was arrested, and she looked again in some surprise. Surely the black hair was not so black as it had been. Was it possible that she was making a mistake, or was it not perceptibly lighter in hue?

As if conscious of her scrutiny the governess flushed uncomfortably, and Barbara dropped her eyes.

"Yes, Maisie and I must certainly pay the mamma pussy a visit after tea," she said gently.

Just then a maid entered with a fresh relay of tea and hot scones. Barbara glanced at her a little curiously.

"Surely that is a new face."

"Yes," Miss Martin assented. "Susan has only been here three days. Eliza, our old maid, had to keep house for her father because her mother died. We were very sorry to lose her, but we think we shall like Susan just as well in time."

"I don't," Maisie said decidedly. "Susan pulls my hair when she is brushing it out at night. Eliza never did."

Miss Martin hushed her into silence just as the maid entered again.

"This letter came for you by the afternoon post, miss," she said to Miss Martin. "Hollins has been into Castor and brought it back with him."

Barbara looked up with interest. Afternoon post was something of a novelty at the Priory, as the letters had to be specially fetched from Castor.

"Are there any for me?" she inquired.

"I don't think so, miss," the maid said primly. "But of course I look after only the schoolroom letters."

Barbara was just about to speak again when she caught sight of the envelope as it lay on the salver that Susan was presenting to Miss Martin.

She could not mistake that bold, black writing—somewhat scrawly. The letter was written by her lover, Frank Carlyn. Involuntarily she glanced from it to the governess. Miss Martin's face was a fiery red, her hand trembled perceptibly as she slipped the letter into her pocket. Some of the glow seemed to spread itself to Barbara's face. She was conscious of a strong thrill of satisfaction that her letter of dismissal to Frank Carlyn had been already written, before she recognized that tell-tale handwriting.

The next moment the door was opened again and Sybil Lorrimer looked in.

"Ah, they told me you were here, Barbara. The Turners have come in and the Rectory children and they want to play games. You are all to come down—you too, please, Miss Martin. We want everybody to play."

"Oh, that will be jolly," Maisie said as she jumped up with all the only child's zest at the prospect of companionship.

She danced off, pulling Sybil with her, Barbara and Miss Martin following more slowly.

The latter's flush had faded now. She looked white and jaded, a little sad too. In the drawing-room they found a merry party assembled engaged in the intellectual occupation of drawing a pig blind-folded, and putting their initials beside their productions.

Maisie and Sybil were absorbed, Barbara went over to Lady Davenant, and the governess quietly sat down in a distant corner hoping to avoid notice.

Presently she became aware that the game had changed, they were playing something with pencil and paper, when somebody produced an album and requested everybody to write his or her favourite verse in it. Elizabeth was wondering whether she might slip away if Lady Davenant would give her permission, when that lady beckoned to her.

"Come, my dear, you must join in this," she said kindly. "Do you know I did not see that you were in the room until Sybil drew my attention to you just now."

"I was about to ask whether I might go away," hazarded the governess doubtfully.

Lady Davenant shook her head. "Oh, no, my dear. You shut yourself up far too much as it is. Now this is really a funny game. You each have a sheet of paper and you damp your thumb on this blue pad and then print it on the paper so—do you see? And put your initials on it, and pass it on to the person on your right and she puts heads and legs to it and makes it into a funny likeness of yourself. We played it last night with Maisie, Sybil and Barbara, and I quite enjoyed it."

Miss Martin looked doubtfully at the piece of paper handed to her.

"Oh, I don't think—"

But Lady Davenant pointed to a seat near Maisie. "Nonsense, my dear, a bit of fun will do you good." The governess had no choice but to obey, though she was longing to get away to read her letter. Like Barbara she had recognized the writing and her amazement had far surpassed the other girl's. She could not imagine what Frank Carlyn could be writing to her about, and her mind was a prey to all sorts of imaginings and surmises.

"Now, Miss Martin," Sybil thrust a pencil and pad into her hand. "Put your right thumb on this, then press it upon the paper—so—initial it, and pass it on." She seated herself on the other side of Elizabeth. "Now is everybody ready? Pass!"

There was some laughter as she was obeyed, and she caught Elizabeth's paper and hurried across to the Turners.

"That is wrong, you must all pass to the right." No one saw her thrust the piece of paper she held in her hand into her little satchel. She came back to her place in a minute and held out her hand to the governess. "Your paper, please, Miss Martin."

"I gave it to you a minute ago," said Elizabeth in surprise.

"Did you?" Sybil questioned. "I don't think you did, or if you did I have lost it. Do you see Miss Martin's paper over there, any of you? No. Oh, just do another, Miss Martin. I must have dropped it somewhere."

Elizabeth obeyed. The game did not strike her as very interesting, and she was only longing to get away. She gave a sigh of unfeigned relief when, the papers having been collected and admired, Mrs. Turner declared it was time to be going, and swept all the party away. But even then she was not free. Sir Oswald sent to ask her to write some letters for him, and her own had to remain unread.

When the last of the guests had gone, Sybil ran lightly upstairs. In her room Susan, the schoolroom maid, was sewing some lace into a frock.

Sybil waved the piece of paper she drew from her satchel in triumph.

"Well, I have managed it, Susan. But it needed a little diplomacy."

The maid took it from her and scrutinized it carefully.

"So this is Miss Martin's thumb-mark, is it?" she said slowly, her eyes narrowing. "Well, now I think I can promise you it won't be long before we have some news for you, Miss Lorrimer."

Chapter Twelve

ALONE at last! Elizabeth closed her door and locked it. It really seemed to her that everyone had been conspiring against her this evening. After Sir Oswald's letters were done, Maisie had been unusually tiresome, and after the child was safely in bed Lady Davenant had paid one of her infrequent visits to the schoolroom, and had stayed chatting pleasantly over many subjects, while Elizabeth had the greatest difficulty in preventing her impatience from becoming visible.

But now it was all over and she was her own mistress until the morning.

She drew the letter from her pocket and scrutinized it carefully. It was undoubtedly Frank Carlyn's writing, she could not fail to recognize it, though the times she had seen it before were very few. The postmark too—she shivered as she looked at it—was Carlyn.

She shivered again as she opened the envelope, the prevision of evil was strong upon her, and she hesitated a moment, glancing round with wide frightened eyes, before she drew out the enclosure. Then, as she looked down, she saw that it was merely the briefest of notes. It began abruptly without any prefix.

"It has come to my knowledge accidentally that Marlowe, the late constable at Carlyn, has been seen in the neighbourhood of the Priory. He is there ostensibly on business, but there may be danger. Be careful." It was signed simply F.C.

She read it through twice, then she looked up feverishly. She had thrown off her disguising glasses and her big, grey eyes were wide and dilated by fear.

"What does it mean?" she sobbed beneath her breath. "What can it mean? Except that the end is drawing near." Then as she glanced downwards, she struck at the letter with her open palm. "Oh, the coward!" she breathed. "The wicked coward!"

She had seated herself in a chair near the dressing-table. As she looked up she caught sight of her reflection in the glass. She paused with the letter in her hand, staring before her with a new fear gripping her heart. Surely she could not be mistaken. The mass of dark hair brushed so smoothly back from her brow was distinctly lighter in colour. There could be no mistake about it; the difference that Barbara had noticed was even more marked now.

Elizabeth thrust the letter back into her pocket as she got up, and going nearer to the dressing-table scrutinized herself more closely. Yes, the change was marked; and yet, only yesterday, fancying that there was some alteration, she had been more careful than usual.

She went over to a box she always kept locked, and unfastening it took out a case containing a bottle half-full of some dark liquid, a saucer, and quite an array of small brushes.

"It cannot be that it is failing now," she murmured. "It has always answered so well hitherto."

She hurried into her dressing-gown and let down her hair. Then, after regarding it for a minute or two with increasing dissatisfaction, she poured some of the liquid from the bottle into the saucer, and taking up one of the brushes began slowly to damp her hair, holding it out from the roots to the tips and going over every bit carefully.

It was a long process, and it was past her usual bedtime when she had finished, but she did not hurry with her undressing; even before Carlyn's letter had come she had been oppressed by a feeling of danger, a feeling that was intensified tenfold now. A strong foreboding was upon her that the day of reckoning was close at hand, try to evade it as she might. That it was likely to prove a heavy day for others as well as for herself she knew only too well, and her heart failed her as she thought of it. Even after she was in bed she lay awake, the livelong night, tossing from side to side, the dread that had been upon her in the day-time increased tenfold in the hours of darkness. Where lay the danger? She could not even guess, and her helplessness deep-ened the mysterious terror that oppressed her.

She remembered Marlowe well, she had little doubt that he would recognize her. She was convinced that his sharp eyes would penetrate her disguise.

Towards morning she fell into an uneasy doze, in which triv-ial things, like Maisie's lessons, mixed themselves up with the dreadful days that had preceded the governess's coming to the Priory. Then her mind recurred to an earlier time still. She was once more the petted darling of her father's house. Her father seemed to be waiting for her, watching her, and she caught the echo of his kindly tones, "Come home, little girl, come home." With this last dream, there mingled, oddly enough, memories of Sir Oswald's love-making, of the tenderness that had grown in his voice when he had spoken of his love for her, when he had begged her to come and be eyes for him in his helplessness.

She woke with a sob in her throat as Susan entered with her tea. The maid placed the tray beside the bed, drew up the blinds, then, with an unseen glance at the long tresses lying on the pillow, departed with a gleam of triumph in her eyes.

Elizabeth sat up in bed and drank her tea feverishly. Now in the clear morning light things did not seem quite so bad. She began to think that she had let her fears exaggerate her danger. After all Marlowe's visit to the neighbourhood might have no connexion with her at all. It might simply be that a malign fate had ordained that he, like Carlyn and Barbara Burford, should have friends in the district. If she kept out of his sight all might be well.

Resolving that, for sometime at any rate, she would not venture out of the Park and its immediate precincts, she sprang out of bed. Then as she faced the long pier glass she uttered a cry of horror. The hair which up to a few days ago had been so black was now only a pale brown; there was no possibility of the change passing unnoticed to-day—it was obvious enough to strike the most casual observer.

But what could have brought it about? She could not imagine. As she hurriedly dressed herself she made up her mind that the only thing she could do was to ask for a day's holiday, go up to Town and see if she could get the hair put right, keeping it in the meantime covered as much as possible. To this end, when the dressing bell rang, she put on her hat and coat and twisted a veil round her hair. Maisie's sharp little eyes and tongue were to be dreaded as much as anything she knew.

Then she begged for an interview with Lady Davenant, who usually kept her room until the middle of the day. She found the old lady in bed and distinctly curious as to the meaning of this early visit.

In spite of everything Elizabeth was not a good liar. She hesitated and stammered so much as she told the story she had decided on that a keener person than Lady Davenant would have guessed that something was amiss at once.

As it was, however, her tale did very well. She had had a letter the preceding afternoon, she said, which necessitated her going up to Town at once. If Lady Davenant would allow her she would take the express at 10.30 and be back that same evening.

Lady Davenant looked a little perplexed by the suddenness of the request.

"If you had told me when you had the letter yesterday," she said plaintively, "then I could have arranged everything. Now what am I to do about Maisie?"

"If she might have a holiday to-day I know that Latimer would look after her, and I could make it up to her later on. I am so sorry, dear Lady Davenant, but yesterday I thought it could be done by letter. Now I see it can't and it is so very important. You see"—her face colouring—"it is so very important that I should take care of my savings, in case my health should fail, or anything."

"Of course it is, my dear." Lady Davenant was easily placated. "Well, you must go. As you say, Latimer can take care of Maisie, and Oswald's letters can wait. Or I daresay Sybil—"

"Who is taking Sybil's name in vain?" that young lady's voice interrupted at this juncture, and Sybil's fair head was popped round the door. "What! Miss Martin, you are an early visitor. Going out already to—" with a glance at the other's hat and veil.

"Oh, Sybil, Miss Martin is going up to Town." Lady Davenant eagerly related Elizabeth's difficulty while the governess sat silent.

Sybil listened, the smile in her eyes deepening as she looked at the governess.

"I do hope you will get your business done successfully," she said amiably. "But you will not have much time to spare if you want to catch the express."

Elizabeth found this was true enough. She had to hurry over her breakfast and her farewells to Maisie, who by no means approved of being left, but she managed to be in time for the train.

The carriage was crowded, but it was a two hours' journey to town; she had plenty of time for reflection in the train; but she little guessed that the shabby-looking man who was apparently asleep at the other end of the carriage was in reality watching her from beneath his lowered eyes, that not a change of expression on her part escaped him.

Still less did she imagine when the train had steamed into the great terminus, and she had engaged a taxi to convey her to her destination, that the same shabby-looking man was in another taxi behind, that his driver had orders not to let her out of sight.

She had given the name and address of an expensive hairdresser's in a quiet little street off Piccadilly. An attendant came forward as she entered the shop.

"I had a preparation from here for tinting the hair a darker shade," Elizabeth began.

The man bowed. "Yes, madam."

"Well, for a time it answered perfectly," Elizabeth told him. "But lately, this last week or so, it has failed. Not only that, but it seems to have an absolutely contrary effect, and the hair seems lighter after each application."

The man looked surprised. "I don't understand that, madam. You are sure you have applied it according to the directions?"

"Quite sure, absolutely," Elizabeth said with conviction. "As I have more than half a bottle of the liquid left, I brought it with me that you might see whether there is anything wrong with it. I have had no reason to complain until the last bottle. Is it a usual thing for the preparation to fail after a certain time?"

The man looked puzzled. "We have never had such a case, madam. If you will allow me to see it perhaps I can find some explanation."

Elizabeth opened her bag and took out the bottle.

"Here it is!" Then she threw back her veil.

"You see it was to make my hair dark, and look at it now."

The man raised his eyebrows as he glanced across. Had Elizabeth but known, it was even lighter than in the morning. He took out the cork and smelt the contents of the bottle, his expression of perplexity deepening, then he poured a little in a saucer and looked at it. Finally he glanced up at Elizabeth.

"If you would not mind waiting a few minutes, madam, I think I can soon tell you what is wrong."

Elizabeth sat down in one of the softly cushioned window seats. She was glad of the rest, for she was becoming aware that her sleepless nights had tired her, while the incessant worry of the past few months had told enormously on her once splendid physique.

The man came back in a shorter time than she had expected.

"It was as I thought, madam. The preparation in your bottle is not that supplied by us."

Elizabeth stared at him. "But it is! Do you not see your name on the bottle? The case is precisely as it came from you."

The man shook his head. "The name, the bottle and the case are all ours, madam, but the preparation has been substituted for ours. It is one of the most powerful bleaching mixtures I know, and so powerful that we should hesitate to employ it ourselves."

A sick feeling of fear was creeping over Elizabeth.

"It can't be, it can't be," she reiterated. "It has been kept locked up always. How could it have been changed?"

The man shrugged his shoulders. "I can't tell, madam. Only assuredly it was not done without hands."

No, Elizabeth saw that. The sickness that was creeping over her seemed to increase, her legs tottered under her. She sat down again suddenly.

"Who could it have been?" she breathed half aloud. "Does somebody suspect? Does somebody know?"

Chapter Thirteen

BARBARA BURFORD was very unhappy, there was no doubt of that. The end of her love dream had been a terrible blow to her, and now to add to it Frank Carlyn was not inclined to take his dismissal quietly. Every post since he had received it had brought her letters from him. He seemed utterly unable to account for or understand the change in her attitude towards him, and his pleading for another trial, or at least for a hearing before his sentence was pronounced, formed only too ready a seconder in Barbara's own treacherous heart. Yet her common sense told her that, knowing what she knew, she would be foolish in the extreme to consent to the renewal of an engagement which it seemed to her could only end in catastrophe. Explanations, too, were difficult, under the circumstances; so far Barbara had only taken refuge in silence. In spite of her father's desire to have her at home she had asked Lady Davenant to keep her a few days longer at the Priory, to enable her to realize things a little and to prepare herself for the battle with her father which she knew would ensue on her return to Carlyn.

With Frank's last letter in her hand she was looking for some place of refuge where she might give herself the luxury of a long, quiet think. Sybil was with Sir Oswald in the study. Barbara peeped into the library—it was empty. It looked very comfortable with the firelight flickering on its capacious armchairs and wide, cushioned window-seats.

Barbara ensconced herself on one of the latter with her head against the woodwork. She had no idea how completely the heavy velvet curtains hid her from the sight of anyone entering the room.

There was nothing very fresh in Frank's letter. It merely reiterated the fact that the feelings of the writer had in no way changed, and begged an interview so that he might convince Barbara that their old friendship had merged into love. Nevertheless as Barbara read it over again her eyes filled with tears. She sat there dreaming over it with misty eyes it seemed to her for hours, until the room grew dark but for the fitful gleams of the firelight, and then, tired out and worried, she fell into a restless doze.

She never knew how long she had been asleep; she did not hear the door open and shut, but at last she was awakened by the sound of voices—Sybil's and another which she did not at first recognize. She was about to get up and speak when she caught a sentence which made her pause.

"So that was why Frank Carlyn recognized her?"

"Of course," answered the other speaker, whom, to her surprise, Barbara, now recognized as Susan, the schoolroom maid. "You remember that it was on his estate that the murder took place."

"Yes, and there was some talk about him and the woman, wasn't there? Well, I don't care if he does get into a bit of trouble too," Sybil said viciously. "It will teach him not to help adventuresses who palm themselves off as governesses in decent people's houses. You are sure there is no mistake?"

"Impossible," Susan said positively. "That thumb-mark you were able to get for us settled matters. Mrs. Winter left one or two such mementoes at the cottage. They are precisely identical."

There was no hesitation in Barbara's mind now: eaves-dropping or no eavesdropping she must hear the end of this conversation. She sat perfectly still, scarcely even daring to breathe. Presently Susan went on again:

"It has been a sore point with my brother ever since that time that Winter's wife escaped. There won't be any mistake this time."

Sybil laughed, a hard, heartless sound that made Barbara shiver. "When are they going to arrest her?"

"Very soon now," the other answered. "They are going to Sir Francis Geyton's for the warrant. They ought to be here within the hour. After all, though the woman doesn't deserve any pity, Miss Lorrimer, I couldn't help feeling a bit sorry for her when I went into the schoolroom just now and saw her sitting there so quiet with Miss Maisie. She little knows what is in store for her to-night."

"I am not sorry for her a bit," Sybil said with a hard laugh. "Do you suppose my cousin would have her to teach his child if he knew that she was a murderess?"

"Well, it has got to be proved yet that she is, you know," Susan remarked cautiously, "though I don't think there is much doubt about it myself."

"Not a bit, I should say," Sybil agreed quickly. "I know Sir Oswald always thought her guilty. It is the irony of fate that he, who took so much interest in that case, should actually have the criminal hiding in his own house. But"—her voice suddenly altering—"what about Mrs. Sunningdale? She recommended her so strongly, and I can't understand—"

"Oh, don't you see that this isn't the Miss Martin who was with Mrs. Sunningdale at all?" Susan interrupted. "That poor thing died in hospital the fortnight before Miss Maisie's govern-ess came to the Priory. She was visited while she was dying by a tall, fair woman, answering to Mrs. Winter's description, and there can be little doubt that when Miss Martin was dead the idea of impersonating her occurred to Mrs. Winter. She might have carried the affair on much longer but for your finding the photograph of her husband which Mr. Gregg recognized and which put him on the right track."

"I was certain from the first that she was an adventuress, and I was determined to expose her." Sybil's tone was full of triumph; not one thought of pity had she for the woman whose doom was so swiftly approaching.

"Who will make the arrest?" she went on. "Your brother?"

"Oh, no, Jim has given up the regular force. Two officers came down from Scotland Yard this morning. It is they who will manage everything now. But, Miss Lorrimer, don't you think some care should be taken that Lady Davenant is not frightened?"

"Oh, yes. I will tell her maid not to let anyone go in to her but Sir Oswald, and myself," Sybil said carelessly. "I wonder what Sir Oswald will say when he knows the truth. I shall enjoy seeing his face."

Susan made a quick movement of repulsion. She was hardened to the hunting down of criminals, but there was something in Sybil's attitude towards the unfortunate governess that revolted her, detective though she was.

She turned to the door. "That is all, then, I suppose, Miss Lorrimer?"

"Yes, I suppose so," Sybil said doubtfully. "You will be watching her until the arrest is made, of course?"

Susan nodded.

"She doesn't want much watching, poor thing; she is sitting as quiet as you please in the schoolroom, with her book. But I am going to put Miss Maisie to bed, and then I can make an excuse to be tidying up and be going in and out and keep an eye on her until they come."

"That is all right, then," Sybil said in a satisfied tone. "The house is watched too, you said?"

Susan nodded. "Oh, yes. And both the lodges. Oh, she is safe enough, don't you fear, Miss Lorrimer."

"Well, we shall meet when the detectives come, I suppose," Sybil said with a light laugh. "Till then—" She opened the door and Barbara heard them both go out of the room.

Left alone, Barbara sat perfectly still for a minute or two, her hands pressed tightly to her forehead, trying to gather her scattered wits together, to realize the sense of what she had heard.

That Sybil should have done as her words implied, that she should have introduced a private detective into her cousin's house in order to spy out the past of a member of his household seemed inconceivably horrible to Barbara. As she dropped her hands they fell on Frank Carlyn's letter lying in her lap; and she started quickly as if she had been stung. What would this news—this arrest mean to him?

She shivered as she pictured the trouble that might be in store for him. A year ago at Carlyn she had refused to believe the gossip that whispered that Frank Carlyn was oftener at his head gamekeeper's cottage than was necessary, and hinted that the latter's pretty wife was the attraction. Yet, deny it as she might, a doubt had rankled in Barbara's mind—a doubt which had changed into something much stronger when she saw the governess at the Priory, and marked the understanding which evidently subsisted between her and Carlyn.

But Barbara's nature was entirely unlike that of Sybil Lorrimer. Not a finger would she have raised to separate Carlyn from the woman she thought he loved. Was it possible that anything could avert the evil that Sybil had wrought, she asked herself. The thought crossed her mind that the governess might make her escape before the officers arrived, but the time was so short, barely an hour, Susan had said. If it had been possible she would have sent for Carlyn, but as it was she could think of no one upon whom she could rely to help the poor, hunted woman upstairs. Of Sir Oswald's feelings towards his child's governess she was in entire ignorance. She had noted Sybil's jealousy and judged it to be quite unfounded as far as she could see. But, even had she known of it, Sir Oswald in his helplessness could not have given her the help she wanted to-night. The house was watched, she had heard, and, even if it were possible to elude the watchers, where could the fugitive go? Unless she had some place of refuge she would inevitably be overtaken and arrested. Barbara's head reeled as she thought of it. But she pulled herself together in a minute. The time was short, the poor thing in the schoolroom must be warned.

The idea crossed Barbara's mind that Mrs. Winter had successfully engineered one escape. Perhaps she might be able to think of something now.

The girl's limbs felt stiff and heavy as she stood up, her head ached violently as she made her way upstairs to the schoolroom. Maisie's bedroom was just down the passage. Knocking at the schoolroom door Barbara could hear the child talking, could catch some of the maid's rejoinders. She shivered as she recalled the girl's promise to Sybil that she would be about the schoolroom until the detectives came.

"Come in!" Miss Martin said in her clear, low voice.

She was, as Susan had said, sitting by her table reading. She looked up in surprise as Barbara opened the door.

"Miss Burford, Maisie has just gone to bed."

"Yes, I know," Barbara said, coming into the room and closing the door very carefully behind her. "I came to see you, not Maisie."

"To see me!" The governess rose and moved forward a chair. "How very kind of you!" she said gratefully.

With a quick motion of her head Barbara declined the chair.

"I came," she began abruptly, then she broke off, her breath catching in her throat with a curious husky sound.

How could she tell this woman confronting her so quietly the tidings she had brought. But there was no time to be lost. After all the simplest words would be the best. She looked away from the governess's surprised face, her eyes following mechanically the antics of Maisie's kitten playing on the hearthrug.

"I came to warn you," she said in a husky tone. "To tell you that I have accidentally learned that you are in great danger, that unless you can manage to make your escape you will be arrested."

"Arrested!" The governess sank back in her chair, her face turned a livid white. She put out her hands imploringly. "Ah, no, no!"

"There is no doubt, I am afraid," Barbara said in the same jerky fashion. "Unless you can think of a way of escape, and there is very little time."

Elizabeth tossed her spectacles on the table. Her grey eyes were full of horror and appeal.

"I—I can't think of anything," she moaned.

"Stay, give me one moment. But I must go at once before they come."

She caught up a garden hat that lay on a chair beside her and began to pin it on. Then she stopped short in bewilderment and stared at the girl in front of her.

"You know?"

"Yes," Barbara said quietly. "I have known ever since I came. I think I recognised you at once."

The big, grey eyes opposite hers were still dilated—fixed upon her.

"And you kept silence—you would help me?" the governess breathed.

"Yes," Barbara said simply. "I want to help you—for Frank Carlyn's sake."

Chapter Fourteen

THERE WAS a moment's tense silence. The governess's face, which until then had been full of feeling, grew suddenly hard and grave, her grey eyes looked cold.

"She must get me out of the way for Frank Carlyn's sake," she said slowly to herself.

"I see," she said aloud. "Yes, it will be awkward for Mr. Carlyn when I am arrested."

Barbara caught her breath quickly.

"But you must not be arrested—for both your sakes. Can't you think of anything—go anywhere?"

"How can I go anywhere?" the woman opposite questioned with white, stiff lips. "I should be watched, followed?"

Barbara clasped her hands. "If I could get you out of the house have you anywhere you could go—where you would be safe?"

The governess did not answer. Her eyes glanced restlessly at the window, through which in the daytime a distant glimpse of the chimneys of Walton Grange could be obtained. In that minute Elizabeth's pride fought a battle at its last stronghold—fought and was vanquished. She was beaten to the very ground now and she knew it. If it were possible to save her there was nothing left for her but the one refuge she had sworn never to claim. She made a weary gesture of surrender and she turned to Barbara.

"Yes, if I could get away from here I think I should be safe."

"Then I have thought of something," Barbara began hurriedly, then she stopped short. There was the loud teuf-teuf of a motor in the drive beneath. "The Turners' car," she exclaimed. "Just what I was hoping for. Algy was to bring me a parcel from town on his way to the station. We are saved."

"How—I don't understand," the governess said helplessly.

"He shall drive you to safety," Barbara said eagerly. "Wait quietly here, Miss Martin. I must go down and explain to him."

"But you can't tell him—he won't—" Elizabeth gasped.

"That will be all right," Barbara assured her. She ran out of the room and downstairs at full speed.

The car was standing before the open door. Young Turner was leaning out talking to the butler.

"Algy, Algy!" she called out. "I want you."

"And I want you," he retorted with a laugh. "I have the new car. Come for a spin and try her—she is a beauty."

All the Turners were fond of Barbara. Algy, the young hope of the house, a boy of twenty, was particularly devoted to her.

"I believe I will," Barbara said gaily, though all her pulses were thrilling with fear. Suppose the detectives came before she was ready? She ran down the steps. "Sure you won't spill me? Oh, she is a beauty. I really can't resist her." Then she cast an anxious look round. The butler was out of ear-shot. If unseen watchers were in the bushes it was impossible that they should catch what she said. Her tone changed.

"Algy, will you help me? I want a friend badly."

"Why, of course I will. You know that, Barbara," young Turner said heartily. "What is it?"

Barbara drew him down to her. "There is some one here to-night who must be got away without anyone knowing. She shall come down to you in a minute dressed in my things. Will you do this for me, Algy?"

"I would do much more than that to help you," young Turner responded warmly. "And this sounds as if it might be jolly fun."

Barbara caught her breath. "It isn't fun at all," she said desperately. "It is dead earnest, and it is only fair to tell you, Algy, that you may get into awful trouble about it. But I don't know who else to turn to. I must have help to-night at once."

"Bless you, don't you worry about trouble for me," Algy laughed. "I'm always in it, more or less, a bit extra will run easily enough off my shoulders. They are broad enough to stand it."

Barbara patted his arm. "You are a good boy," she said gratefully. "Then I will send her downstairs to you at once. You understand, Algy. You will pretend she is me, and you will be ready to start as soon as she comes, in case anyone should try to stop you."

"I should be sorry for them if they tried to interfere with my new car," Algy said grimly. "That is all right, Barbara. Nobody shall stop me between here and the lodge and I will drive your friend wherever she wants to go."

Your friend! The irony of that expression almost made Barbara smile. But she sprang back and ran up the steps.

"Only half an hour and you will have to bring me back safely," she called out gaily.

"Oh, I will bring you back all right," Algy promised cheerfully. "Don't you be half an hour putting your coat on, Barbara."

"I won't be a minute," the girl assured him laughingly.

In the hall she paused a moment, yet there was a good deal to be done and not much time to do it. There were two people who must be got out of the way for the next ten minutes, Sybil Lorrimer and the schoolroom maid. It was fairly easy to Barbara's fertile brain to think of a way to get rid of Sybil. She tapped at the door of the study.

"Oswald, don't you want any letters written to-night?"

"No, I don't think so, thanks," Sir Oswald answered, raising his head in some surprise.

"Oh, but you must!" Barbara contradicted.

"Anyhow, I wish you would ask Sybil to write some for you. I want to be sure that she is quietly in here for the next half-hour."

Sir Oswald laughed. "If it is to oblige you," he began. Then blind though he was, he seemed to divine some of the real anxiety that underlay the lightness of the girl's tone. "I have rather an important letter that I was going to ask Miss Martin to answer for me," he said quietly. "But I daresay Sybil would be kind enough to do it instead."

"I am sure she would," Barbara agreed with a sigh of relief. "And you will send for her at once, Oswald? You will ask her to do it now?"

"Instantly." Sir Oswald touched the bell. "Will that satisfy you, Barbara?"

"Thank you very much," the girl said gratefully. She hurried out into the hall, almost running into Sybil Lorrimer as she did so.

"Why are you in such a hurry?" that young lady inquired. "Is that Algy Turner outside? I want to speak to him."

Such a desire on Sybil's part had never occurred to Barbara; for a moment she thought her whole scheme might be wrecked. Then she said quickly, "Do keep him patient while I put on my coat, I am going for a spin in his new car. Oswald wants some one to write a letter for him. Do you know whether Miss Martin is in the schoolroom?"

"I don't know." Sybil turned back on her way to the front door. "Don't bother about her, I will go to Oswald."

Barbara ran upstairs. There was still the schoolroom-maid to be disposed of, and this might be a more difficult matter than getting Sybil out of the way. Nothing had occurred to her when outside the passage leading to the schoolroom apartments she met Latimer. Barbara had earned for herself a very warm place in Latimer's heart. The maid had been devoted to Sir Oswald's young wife, and she did not forget the warm friendship that had subsisted between the two girls.

Barbara took quick counsel with herself. Latimer could give her the help she craved.

"Latimer," she said quickly, "I want to have a little talk with Miss Martin, just a little private talk, and I am sure that the new schoolroom-maid, Susan, listens. Could you—"

"I am not at all sure that you are not right, miss," was Latimer's unexpected rejoinder. "It seems to me the girl is always poking and prying about. If I can do anything for you, miss—"

"You could do this, Latimer," Barbara said smilingly, earnestly putting her hand on the woman's arm. "Susan is putting Miss Maisie to bed, but she keeps making excuses to come into the schoolroom. If you have a quarter of an hour to spare could you go up and help with Miss Maisie's undressing and keep the door shut and Susan in the room? I will explain all to-morrow. I can't to-night."

"Bless you, miss, I don't want any explanations," Latimer said heartily. "I shall be glad enough of the chance of going through Miss Maisie's wardrobe. Her ladyship said the other day it ought to be done. And I won't give Miss Susan much time for looking after what don't concern her. I can promise you that."

"You are a jewel, Latimer," and the girl gave her arm an affectionate pat.

She heard Maisie's bedroom door shut with a decisive bang before she went into the schoolroom.

The governess was sitting in a huddled up heap in the chair by the fireplace. She lifted up a white, terrified face, her great grey eyes glancing fearfully from side to side.

"Have they come for me?" she questioned hoarsely.

"Come? No," Barbara said, "and long before they come you will be safe away. I told you I had thought of a plan."

She briefly related her arrangement with young Turner. Then she drew the governess into her own room.

"Put on this short, plain coat," she said hurriedly. "And this close-fitting hat; you are to wear my big dust-coloured motoring coat over it all, and turn the collar up, do you see? Then when you get out of the car leave the coat with Algy and you will look quite different. Now all you have to do is to run downstairs as quickly as you can and get into the car. Algy will manage everything else."

Elizabeth's face was muffled up so that it was not easy to see that she was not Barbara, and the big, light motoring coat was known to all the household. Barbara pushed her to the door.

"Be quick! Be quick! You must go alone, and remember that everything depends on you now."

The other girl paused a moment, then she stooped and pressed her hot, fevered lips to the little hands that had been working so hard for her.

"I must thank you and bless you for all you have done for me," she said brokenly. "Even though I know that it was for his sake."

Then she turned very quickly and drawing the cloak more closely round her ran lightly down the stairs. None of Barbara's plans miscarried. Sybil Lorrimer and Susan were neither of them to be seen, and the footman who held the door open was giving all his attention to the car.

Algy made an admirable accomplice. Directly he caught sight of the figure on the stairs he called out in his cheerful, boyish tones: "Now then, Barbara, hurry up. I thought you were only going to be a minute. I like your idea of time."

He sprang out of the car and helped her in, then, taking his place beside her, in a trice they were spinning down the drive.

Barbara, in her own room, standing by the window from which she dared not lift the blind, drew a deep breath of relief as she heard them reach the lodge gates, and knew they had not been stopped. Now, provided that Elizabeth could reach the refuge she had spoken of so confidently, she was safe.

At any rate Barbara could do no more. With a sudden realization of the past hour she sank into the sofa that was drawn up before the fire. She drew out Frank Carlyn's letter again. Less than ever did Carlyn seem to belong to her now, and yet the feeling that she had been doing something for him gave her a strange sense of peace.

She was still lying there, with her hands pressed over her eyes, and trying to still the intolerable aching of her temples, when she heard the sound of a car in the drive. In a moment she realized what it meant. Elizabeth had not escaped a moment too soon. The detectives were here.

She waited for the summons to the front door, but the car turned to the side, to a door that was used mainly by Sir Oswald's tenants and people coming to see him on business. Then Barbara caught the sound of an authoritative knock, she heard the bell ring clearly.

Chapter Fifteen

FOUR MEN got out of the car that had drawn up at the side door of the Priory, Mr. Marlowe, a couple of officers from Scotland Yard, and a man in plain clothes.

Mr. Marlowe had his hand on the knocker when one of the Scotland Yard men stopped him.

"One moment, Marlowe. You must ask for Sir Oswald first. In common courtesy we must explain matters to him before we make an arrest in his house."

"As you please, of course," Marlowe said sullenly. "But you must remember that she is a very cute one, inspector."

Inspector Church of Scotland Yard permitted his grim face to relax in a smile.

"She will be cute if she escapes us now, Mr. Marlowe."

The young footman who answered the door looked surprised at being confronted by four men. Inspector Church and Mr. Marlowe stepped inside.

"We wish to speak to Sir Oswald Davenant," the inspector said authoritatively.

The man looked uncertain. "I am not sure that Sir Oswald is disengaged."

"Please say that Inspector Church, of Scotland Yard, would be glad to see him on important business," was the inspector's response. "My men will wait here," he added, motioning them inside the hall.

The man went away with a scared face and presently returned saying that Sir Oswald would see them.

They found him alone in his study, but the letters on the table and one only half written on the blotter showed that his secretary had only just left him.

The inspector's keen eyes took in so much at a glance. He began at once.

"I am here on unpleasant business, Sir Oswald." Sir Oswald was standing on the hearthrug with his back to the fireplace. "I am sorry to hear it," he said quietly. "What is it, inspector?"

The inspector judged it best to come to the point at once.

"You have in your employment as governess to Miss Davenant a Miss Martin, Sir Oswald."

"Certainly." Sir Oswald's tone grew perceptibly colder. "But I do not understand."

"I hold a warrant for her arrest," the inspector went on rapidly. "I am sorry to have to execute it in your house, Sir Oswald, but I have no choice."

"For Miss Martin's arrest," Sir Oswald repeated in a tone of stupefaction. For one moment he really did not think he could have heard aright. "What do you say?" he demanded. "Whose arrest?"

"Miss Martin's," the inspector repeated stolidly. "Leastways the young woman who has passed here as such. Perhaps it will save time, Sir Oswald, if I tell you at once that I hold a warrant for the arrest of Elizabeth Winter, alias Martin, for the murder of her husband, John Winter, in May of last year."

Sir Oswald stood for a moment as if stunned, then, for the time oblivious of his blindness, he made a hasty step forward.

"You must be mad," he said hoarsely. "How dare you come here and make so infamous a charge?"

"Well, if there is any mistake about it, Sir Oswald, the lady has only got to prove it," the inspector rejoined.

He had expected a considerable amount of surprise on Sir Oswald's part, but he had not been prepared for this agitation. His trained eye saw at once that some strong feeling must be behind, and he recognized that it might make his task one of more difficulty.

"I am sure no one will be better pleased than I shall if she turns out to be innocent," he went on. "If you will kindly allow us to see her, Sir Oswald—"

"Impossible," Sir Oswald exclaimed. He really hardly knew what he was saying. That such a charge should be brought against the woman he had learned to love, who was daily becoming dearer, more necessary to him, was preposterous, unheard of. Not for one instant did he believe that there was the smallest ground for it; but, out of the general feeling of chaos it engendered, one idea formulated itself. If such an accusation were brought against Elizabeth, at least she should not meet it alone. He would stand by her side, he would proclaim his love and belief in her to the world.

"If you have to see Miss Martin, it must be in my presence," he said haughtily. "I could not allow her to meet such an absurd charge alone. If you still persist in it, I will ask her to come here, she shall know how utterly I disbelieve it."

The inspector bowed.

"As you please, Sir Oswald. I have no choice but to make the arrest."

"It is a monstrous thing," Sir Oswald said, his right hand clenched and taut, the muscles showing hard through the tightening skin. The impulse to throw the inspector and his man out of the house was strong upon him, but his common sense told him that any attempt to prevent the execution of the warrant now would only recoil upon Elizabeth.

He rang the bell.

"Ask Miss Martin if she will be good enough to come here for a minute," he said to the man who appeared with remarkable celerity.

There was an awkward interval while they waited. Sir Oswald leant against the mantelpiece, stern and forbidding-looking. The inspector regarded his finger-nails with much interest, and Mr. Marlowe fidgeted about from one foot to the other, keeping his eyes on the door meanwhile. He had time to grow exceedingly restless, even Sir Oswald was obviously listening impatiently when at last steps were heard returning.

"If you please, Sir Oswald," the footman said, opening the door. "Miss Martin is not in the schoolroom and we can't find her, nobody knows where she is."

Sir Oswald, who had made a step forward, fell back. With a smothered imprecation Marlowe sprang forward.

"Escaped us again, by Heaven!" he cried. "This is your doing"—turning fiercely to the inspector—"while we have been fooling here she has got away."

"She cannot have got out of the house," the inspector said quietly. He turned to Sir Oswald. "You will understand, Sir Oswald, we must search the house at once. Mrs. Winter has successfully eluded us for so long that we are not taking any risks now."

"I do not acknowledge that Miss Martin is Mrs. Winter," Sir Oswald said firmly. "In fact I am positive that you are making an egregious mistake which Miss Martin will explain directly. In the meantime I cannot interfere with you." With a gesture of impatience he turned away.

His heart was bitter within him. It seemed that he could do nothing for the woman he loved. His helplessness had never pressed more heavily upon him. He could not even go about the house, find her before the detectives did, and protect and reassure her; he could only wait and trust that she would come to him for refuge. He purposely left the study door open and various sounds from the hall reached him. Marlowe and Church were not inclined to let the grass grow under their feet, but it was soon evident that the governess was not in the schoolroom or in her room, was not in any of her usual haunts, and an uneasy fear began to dawn upon the inspector that for the second time they had been outwitted.

Susan, released by Latimer, came to join them, hearing from the confusion what had happened. Her brother turned upon her angrily.

"Here's a pretty kettle of fish! Didn't I tell you not to let the woman out of your sight until we came?"

Susan was looking white and puzzled. "She was in the school-room not a quarter of an hour ago, sitting as quiet as could be with her book. She couldn't have got away. It is impossible."

"Possible or not, you mark my words, she has done it," Marlowe said gloomily. They were coming downstairs now. "How did she find out we were after her?" he went on. "There was nobody had any suspicion of it here but you and Miss Lorrimer, was there?"

"No, and Miss Lorrimer was safe enough," Susan said with a wry smile. "She would have moved heaven and earth to have Miss Martin caught if she could. Oh, well we shall get her directly, there is no doubt of that. She must have seen you outside and guessed what was up, and hidden herself somewhere."

"Well, she isn't in the house, is she?" Marlowe questioned roughly.

"I don't think so," Susan said a little doubtfully. "But it is difficult to make sure in a big place like this, and we haven't had long to look. But, if she isn't, she must be in the park or garden. Who is this?"

"This" proved to be one of Inspector Church's men who had been stationed outside. He looked bewildered as he blinked his eyes in the bright light of the hall.

"Please, sir, I was stationed at the gates and I thought I had better tell you that a motor went out just a few moments before you came."

"Yes?" The inspector questioned sharply. "Who was in it, man?"

"Only young Mr. Turner and Miss Burford, the young lady who is stopping here, leastways there was nobody else to be seen."

"Miss Burford!" Susan echoed, her eyes very wide open. "But Miss Burford is in her room. She answered just now when I asked her about Miss Martin, and said she did not know where she was."

Marlowe struck his hands together.

"That is how we have been done," he cried.

"Or, stay, is it possible that it was the other, in Miss Burford's room, answering for her?"

Susan sprang towards the stairs. "I will soon make sure."

Her brother hurried after her, and waited at the end of the passage while she went on to Barbara's room.

Susan unconsciously knocked authoritatively. The room appeared to be in darkness, her heart beat high with the hope that perhaps Jim had been right, after all.

There was no response for a minute; she was just making up her mind to turn the handle and enter when the door was thrown suddenly open, the room was flooded with electric light. Barbara stood upon the threshold.

"What do you want, Susan?" she questioned haughtily. "This is the second time you have been to my room."

"We can't find Miss Martin," Susan said hastily. "And we want her most particularly."

As she spoke Barbara moved quickly down the passage and confronted Marlowe at the end.

"What are you doing here?" she demanded.

"Looking for Miss Martin," the man returned stolidly. "Or as you and I would know her better—by her own name, Miss Burford—for Mrs. Winter, the gamekeeper's wife from Carlyn."

"Absurd!" Barbara said scornfully. "And why are you looking for her in my room, may I ask?"

"Because we heard that you were out motoring with young Mr. Turner," replied Susan who was not to be easily daunted.

"But perhaps those that told us so made a mistake," she finished significantly.

"I promised to go out with Mr. Turner but I changed my mind," she said coldly. She passed the brother and sister and went quickly down to the hall. Her plot had succeeded. Now she was wondering what penalty she would have to pay.

On the mat near the hall door stood Inspector Church and another man talking to Sir Oswald. The inspector had rightly divined what had become of the fugitive, he was withdrawing his men from the Priory, and with the aid of the telephone and telegraph they were hoping to make a successful capture at one of the railway stations within reach.

Meanwhile he was elaborately apologizing to Sir Oswald for having disturbed the Priory in the exercise of his warrant.

Sybil came out of the boudoir. It was evident that she was in a towering temper. Unmindful of the group near the door she swept across to the Marlowes.

"So I hear that you have let her escape again," she said angrily. "This is your fault"—looking at Susan—"I will—"

"Beg pardon, miss, I don't know that it is anyone's fault," Marlowe interrupted. He had recovered his stolidity, telling himself that the unhappy woman would soon be overtaken and arrested. "Of course no one reckoned on Miss Burford helping her to get off."

For an instant Sybil stared at him in amazement; then a light broke upon her; she struck her hands together.

"Barbara! I might have known. But she shall tell us—she shall explain. Barbara!" She raised her voice.

But with a little gesture of infinite scorn Barbara passed her by. At the same moment a grasp of iron was laid on Sybil's arm, and she found herself face to face with Sir Oswald.

"Come here!" he said imperatively, turning back to the library.

Sybil obeyed meekly. Some look in the blind man's face cowed her, and her anger died down.

Sir Oswald closed the door behind them.

"Is it possible that I have heard aright?" he demanded sternly. "Possible that you have introduced a detective into my house, to spy upon a lady who was in possession of my fullest confidence?"

Sybil felt a momentary twinge of shame.

"It was for your sake I did it, Oswald," she said. Then, gathering up her courage, "she was deceiving you all. She is an adventuress, a murderess!"

Sir Oswald held up his hand. "No more of that, Sybil. You are a poor judge of character. Elizabeth Martin a murderess! If the whole world proclaimed her guilty I should know she was innocent. I should like to tell you that a fortnight ago I asked Miss Martin to be my wife, and she refused. If I had been able to see her to-night I should have renewed my offer."

"What!" Sybil's face flushed, and a crimson wave swept over it. "You must be mad, Oswald!" she said hotly. "Quite, quite mad!"

"Possibly," Sir Oswald agreed quietly. "But you will find there is some method in my madness, Sybil. In the meantime you will understand that your visit here must close." He opened the door and bowed to her ceremoniously. "I am sorry my mother will not be able to see you again. After breakfast to-morrow, which no doubt you will wish to take in your own room, I will tell Jones to bring round the car at once."

Chapter Sixteen

ELIZABETH's pulses thrilled as the car swept her down the park to safety. It was not a pleasant night. The moon shone fitfully, but there were heavy banks of clouds, little scuds of moisture blew in her face. Young Turner wrapped her round in rugs. He went on talking to her as if she were Barbara in his frank, breezy way until they were clear of the Priory, and its surrounding trees, then when they were in the open park nearing the lodge gates his tone changed.

"Tell me where you want me to drive you," he said quietly. "I will take you as far as you like. Remember I want to help you for Barbara's sake."

"Thank you," Elizabeth said in a stifled whisper; she thought a moment. "You know the Brangwyn Beech on the Oakover road?"

Algy nodded. "Of course."

"Then," Elizabeth said slowly, "if you will put me down there I shall be most grateful."

Young Turner stared at her blankly. "But that is only five miles away. You don't realize that the car could take you a hundred and never turn a hair—the beauty."

Elizabeth's stiff lips tried to smile.

"Nevertheless, if you put me down near the Brangwyn Beech, provided we are not followed, I am safe."

"Well, you know best, but it doesn't seem much of a start," Algy said ruefully. At the sound of the approaching motor a woman had run out to open the lodge gates. As they glided through Algy called out cheerfully, "Good night, Mrs. Hatchard, unless you like to come with us for a ride."

The woman laughed as she stood back. Algy put on speed as soon as they were on the high road. His quick ears had caught the sound of a car bowling quickly along from the opposite direction towards the Priory.

"Just in time," he said to his companion.

"You mean?" Elizabeth breathed.

Algy turned round. "They have gone up to the Priory. Yes, I fancy those are the people we want to avoid. I say, I am going to drive round a bit before I take you to the Brangwyn Beech. I don't mean the beggars to be able to make sure which way we have gone."

A deep-drawn breath was his only answer. Elizabeth sat motionless; the thought of that car and its occupants paralysed her.

But at last the Brangwyn Beech was reached. Elizabeth threw off the coat. In her black jacket and small, dark hat she looked quite a different person.

Young Turner helped her down and held out his hand.

"Good-bye; I wish you would have let me take you farther."

"This is best, thanks!" Elizabeth said softly, letting her hand rest in his for a minute. "Believe me, I am very grateful to you." Then with a little gesture of farewell she turned away behind the car and was lost to sight amid the darkness.

Algy started without a backward look. He would not pry to find out which way the poor thing had gone, he said to himself. Nevertheless there was a footpath across the moor that ran by the Brangwyn Beech; a shrewd suspicion that that was the way she would take crossed his mind, and he hoped that she knew her way, for Brangwyn moor was not the place to be lost in late at night.

Elizabeth walked on as quickly as she could, stumbling every now and then over the irregularities of the ground. A walk of a couple of miles lay before her, but only the first part was over the moor, very soon she branched off and came to a low stone wall with outstanding steps on either side, Welsh fashion. She clambered over without much difficulty, waited for a moment to recover her breath and then hurried on as if Inspector Church and his myrmidons had been at her very heels. Dark though it was she found her way with very little trouble. It lay now beside shallow stream and the hedge on the other hand and the sound of trickling water guided her. But as she got farther on and found herself in a wood, it was a very different matter.

More than once she ran into tree-trunks, the bushes caught her skirts and tore them. Worse than all, it was beginning to rain in real earnest now, and the rising wind beat it full in Elizabeth's face. It twisted her skirts round her and impeded her progress. It caught strands of her hair and blew them in her cheeks like whipcords. She felt a deplorable object on emerging from the wood, as she realized that she had nearly reached her destination. Before her, only visible in the darkness as a dim intangible shape, stood a moated Elizabethan house—Walton Grange.

Elizabeth knew it at once; on one of her rare holidays from Maisie she had made her way here and gazed at the house from the outside.

She waited a minute trying to gather up her courage. What was she going to say? Then a new terror assailed her. She had no idea of the time, she knew that it must be getting late; suppose the household had retired to bed?

As this fresh notion struck her she brushed back her hair with a weary gesture and started forward again. The footpath she was on led to the grounds of the Grange by a little wicket-gate and a small rustic bridge over the moat. As far as Elizabeth could see the front of the house was all in darkness. She stood still with consternation, and yet she hardly knew that she had intended, certainly not to ring the front door bell. But perhaps on the other side there might be some light. She went round slowly, feeling her way with outstretched hands. Then suddenly she was almost dazed by a blaze of light. A French window stood wide open and through it Elizabeth could see a charming, homelike room. At a davenport in the centre Lady Treadstone sat writing.

Now that everything seemed so easy Elizabeth's courage failed her, she drew back and leaned against the wall, fighting vainly to keep back the sobs that threatened to stifle her.

At last Lady Treadstone got up and came to the window, putting out her hand as though to shut it.

Elizabeth felt that if she did not speak now her last chance would be gone. She stepped forward unsteadily.

"I—I have come—" she began hoarsely, but the words died away in a stifled moan.

"Rosamond!"

Lady Treadstone stood as if petrified for a moment, then with a swift outward movement she caught the poor, shivering creature in her arms.

"Why, Rosamond!" she cried, and there was the sound of tears in her voice. "You have come home at last—Daddy's little Rose!"

She drew the girl in, then very quickly she closed the window and pulled down the blind. Rosamond stood numb and dazed, the change to the warmth and light, after the long cold walk in the darkness and rain, literally dazzled her, and the terror of the nearness of her escape was upon her. She put up her hands to her throat and swayed as she stood.

In an instant Lady Treadstone had caught her and guided her to the big couch before the fire.

"Poor little Rosamond," she said as she laid her down among the cushions. "If you had only trusted me sooner, my dear—but you have come at last, that is all that counts."

Rosamond made a desperate attempt to recall her wandering senses. She knew that there was much that she must tell—must explain. She opened her grey eyes, her lips quivered piteously.

"You knew—when you came to the Priory?" she said with little gasps between each word.

Lady Treadstone was busy taking off her hat and removing her damp jacket. She stooped and kissed the damp cheek.

"Knew!" she echoed. "Ah, yes, I knew you were Daddy's little Rose. That was why I came here—why I took the Grange. I wanted to be near you. Some day I felt you would come home!"

Rosamond began to sob. "Home," she echoed. "Ah, if only I had known sooner!"

"Daddy left you in my charge," Lady Treadstone went on, speaking in low caressing tones as to a child. "He said to me just at the last, 'You will look after Rosamond, and when she comes home tell her her father always loved her. He never forgot his little girl.'"

Rosamond's tears fell thick and fast as she buried her face among the cushions.

"Ah, daddy, daddy!" she sobbed.

"He would have been so happy to-night," Lady Treadstone said gently. "Nay, he is so happy! I am sure he knows, Rosamond!"

In the midst of her tears Rosamond tried to think again, there was something she must tell Lady Treadstone before this sledge-hammer pain in her temples made the telling impossible.

Then she tried to raise herself, to free herself from the encircling arms.

"I—it isn't coming home," she faltered. "I have come for help—refuge. They are looking for me. I am not safe anywhere," looking round wildly. "They want to take me to prison. They say I killed John."

Lady Treadstone's face did not alter. Her hands still touched the girl gently, pitifully.

"You poor little girl," she said softly. "I know all about it, Rosamond, and to whom should you go for help but to me? You will be quite safe here, dear."

"But how—how—?"

"I will tell you," Lady Treadstone said quietly. "Your friend, Miss Martin, wrote to me before she died and told me all. She was frightened at the end when she thought of the mad scheme she had evolved with you, and she begged me to help and save you. I was abroad when her letter came, or I should have tried to do something sooner. But when I did find you, you were not an easy person to help. I could only take this house and wait and watch. I shall always be thankful to Miss Martin."

Rosamond tried to raise herself from the luxurious cushions. She tried to think, but nothing came coherently. She was only conscious that she was tired, so tired. Nevertheless she made one more effort.

"You know I am sorry—that I have repented—" she whispered.

For answer Lady Treadstone bent and kissed her.

"Dear Rosamond, yes. Now you are to forget the past and only remember that you are home again."

She moved a few steps away. Rosamond caught her skirt.

"You are not going?"

"No, no!" Lady Treadstone said caressingly. "I am only going to send for some one who will be almost as pleased to see you as I am." She rang the bell as she spoke. "Greyson—you remember Greyson?—she is with me still, and she has been waiting for you too. I think we shall want her help to-night."

"Greyson!" Rosamond repeated beneath her breath. "Dear Greyson!"

Lady Treadstone waited silently until the door opened and an elderly woman appeared who looked inquiringly at her mistress.

Greyson looked a typical servant of the old school. She wore a gown of black cashmere, very fine and soft, and her cambric apron was edged with the daintiest frills that her own capable hands had goffered and got up. Her pleasant comely face was a little puzzled as Lady Treadstone motioned her to come in, and told her to close the door.

"Look here, Greyson. Some one you know has come home at last," she said, moving aside.

Greyson gazed inquiringly at the woman who was half-lying, half-crouching on the couch, at the masses of dark hair.

"Some one I know, my lady?" she repeated in a bewildered tone. Then as she caught sight of Lady Treadstone's expression, her own changed, she turned back to the couch and took another glance this time at the delicate features, at the tear-filled eyes. The incredulity in her face gave way first to suspicion then to certainty. She sprang forward and caught the trembling figure in her arms.

"Missie! Missie! Come home at last Oh, if my lord had only lived to see the day!" she cried, cradling the girl against her shoulder as though she had still been the child she had nursed. Rosamond felt a vague sense of comfort as she nestled into the resting place where all her childish troubles had been brought.

Lady Treadstone's eyes were wet as she watched them. But presently she touched Greyson's arm.

"Come, Greyson, there is a great deal to be done yet. No one must know that Miss Rosamond is here. I suppose the room leading out of mine is ready?"

Greyson looked up. "Yes, my lady, as you bade me always keep it for Missie."

"That is all right, then." Lady Treadstone took Rosamond's hand. "Now, darling, we will put you to bed there, and I will have a bad cold, and Greyson shall wait upon us both. No one can get to you except through my room, you will be quite, quite safe."

"But supposing they find out that I am here, they follow me?" Rosamond questioned, with dilated eyes. "You cannot bear it. There will be trouble, disgrace."

"Will there?" Lady Treadstone stooped over her. "I don't think they will, but if they do—well, I can bear worse than that for your dear father's sake and your own."

Chapter Seventeen

PORTHCAWEL was at its best in the springtime. Its thatched, irregularly-built cottages were sheltered in the gully that slanted down to the sea, the many coloured creepers on their walls were putting forth tiny tentative tendrils long before there was any sign of life among the gardens for miles along the coast. The hardy daffodils made a golden glory of Porthcawel street before they were even in bud on the headland, where later on they would gleam like patches of sunlight.

Coming suddenly upon Porthcawel after some miles of bleak, uninteresting scenery, Sir Oswald Davenant with his newly-re-covered eyesight thought it the prettiest place he had ever seen. He liked the picturesque freshness of the whitewashed fisher-men's cottages, the quaintness of the cobbled streets up which the donkeys were slowly drawing their loads of fish, above all he loved the glimpse of rippling water at the foot of the cliff and the rocky island that stood out beyond.

"Garth," he said, turning to his companion, a bright-faced boy of twenty or thereabouts. "I think we will make this our headquarters for a day or two if we can find anywhere that will do for the car.

The recovery of his eyesight had worked wonders for Sir Oswald. He looked years younger, his face had regained its vital-ity and energy, he was much thinner and his figure looked alert.

More than a year had elapsed since the tragic disappear-ance of Elizabeth Martin from his house, and as far as he was concerned it remained inexplicable still. The detectives were nonplussed also, apparently. For months Sir Oswald had been afraid to open a paper lest it might contain the tidings of her arrest, but of late another dread had assailed him; he feared that in getting away from her pursuers the governess had come to some harm, fallen into some pool, or perhaps some disused coalpit, and that the body was lying there still undiscovered.

He had undertaken this motor tour with his cousin, Garth Davenant, partly in the hope of distracting his thoughts and attention from that one absorbing subject.

Of Sybil Lorrimer he had refused to hear anything since the discovery of her treachery. Her letters he returned to her unread.

There had been no renewal of the engagement between Barbara and Frank Carlyn. Barbara was still at Carlyn, and more than ever under the ban of Mrs. Carlyn's displeasure, since three months before Frank had departed to Africa with a big game shooting expedition. His mother persisted in regarding him as broken-hearted and Barbara as the cause of it all, and sent the girl to Coventry accordingly. It was very hard upon the girl and she was growing pale and thin, a contrast to the Barbara who had visited the Priory in the first flush of her engagement.

Lady Davenant remained at the Priory. It had been impossible to conceal from her all that had occurred, and she had been greatly shocked and shaken at the time both by the discovery of Sybil's treachery and Miss Martin's duplicity. In a little while, however, with her usual sweetness, she would have forgiven them both and even welcomed Sybil's return had Sir Oswald permitted it.

Another governess had replaced Elizabeth, but her little pupil was still loyal to Miss Martin's memory. No fairy tales were quite as good as hers; no one knew how to make lessons quite so attractive.

Sir Oswald and his cousin got out of their car and looked around. The descent into Porthcawel was far too steep for any motor and there were few dwellings about; a little search, however, revealed a few labourers at work and one of them knew of a shed which might serve as a temporary garage. It turned out all that he promised, and Sir Oswald and Garth turned their attention to the exploration of Porthcawel itself. Its aspect pleased them more and more as they made their way down the rough, uneven steps of the one village street. There was no such thing as apartments to let in Porthcawel, but they were told that it was possible they might get rooms at the "Fisherman's Rest," a primitive inn facing the beach. It happened that the spare rooms were empty. The smiling landlady told them so as she took them upstairs to look at them; long low-raftered apartments with white dimity covered beds redolent of lavender and with the fresh sea air blowing in at the open window.

The two cousins felt that they were in luck as they sat down to their luncheon in the little bar parlour which was as clean and fresh as hands could make it, while the sea breeze gave them an excellent appetite for the fish and home-cured bacon with delicious butter and brown bread.

The landlady was quite a character evidently. She pottered in and out, waiting on them herself, giving them bits of local information the while.

Garth looked at the island, which seemed to rise like a rock sheer out of the sea; round its summit the sea-birds were flying and screeching.

"Is it possible to get over there?" he asked.

"Not that side, sir," the landlady laughed. "I shouldn't fancy there was foothold for a sparrow there, but round to the right of the bay it is different. That is Porthcawel Rock; you may have heard tell of it. They have had pictures of it in some of the papers time back. The house is old and rare they say."

"House? Is there a house there?" Sir Oswald questioned in some surprise.

"Dear me, yes, sir." The landlady answered, evidently astonished at his ignorance. "That is Porthcawel Hold, one of the biggest houses in the country. It belongs to the Treadstones."

"To the Treadstones?" Sir Oswald echoed, struck by the name. "Why, Lady Treadstone, the widow of the late lord, had a house near us for some time. Awfully nice woman she was too," he added. He had always liked Lady Treadstone. Her pleasant voice and manner had attracted him from the first and her evident liking for the lost Elizabeth had won his heart. But she had left Walton Grange some time before he recovered his sight, and he had heard nothing of her since.

"She is living at the Hold now, sir, my lady is," the landlady went on volubly. It was evident from her tone that her respect for her new customer was considerably increased by his acquaintance with Lady Treadstone. "She has been there for the best part of the year, she and Miss Treadstone."

"Miss Treadstone? Ah, I don't know her. She wasn't at Walton," Sir Oswald said easily. "But I remember hearing Lady Treadstone speak of a daughter once."

"Stepdaughter, sir," the landlady corrected. "My late lord was twice married and he and Miss Treadstone used often to be at the Hold in the old days before my second lady was ever thought of. But she has done her duty by Miss Rosamond, my lady has," she concluded judicially. "And I have heard Miss Treadstone herself say she was as fond of her as if she had been her mother really."

Sir Oswald rose and strolled over to the window.

"I think I shall go over to the Hold and call on Lady Tread-stone. I suppose there is some wry of getting there?"

"Only by the sea, sir. And, begging your pardon but her lady-ship don't see any visitors except by invitation. She and Miss Treadstone came here for perfect quiet."

"Oh, well, then!" Sir Oswald shrugged his broad shoulders with an odd feeling of disappointment. "We must amuse our-selves in some other way, I suppose. What do you say to a sail, Garth?"

"Capital," the young fellow exclaimed with boyish enthusi-asm. "There are some decent boats over there too."

"As good as you will find anywhere, sir," the landlady told him with honest enthusiasm. "The Porthcawel fleet isn't to be beaten easily."

"Well, we will have a look at it," Sir Oswald said, strolling to the door. But he was looking at Porthcawel Rock. It seemed to possess a sort of eerie fascination for him.

They got a rowing boat without much difficulty, though the boatman seemed a little doubtful about trusting them alone, and gave them a good deal of advice about his craft's manage-ment and the direction of the currents, advice which somewhat amused Garth, who had rowed in his eight at college.

"If we were the greatest duffers going we couldn't come to harm in a sea like this," he laughed as they got in.

"It don't do to trust too much to that, sir," the old man said. "The wind is rising and we have some sudden storms at this time of the year. This is a nasty bit of coast, you know. But the boat is a good one and if you know how to manage her and humour her a bit you'll do."

He stepped back and Sir Oswald and Garth bent themselves to their oars.

They passed Porthcawel Rock and Sir Oswald saw that there was a little landing-stage, and caught a glimpse through the trees and rocks of the Hold itself. But there was something lonely and chill about it. He wondered that Lady Treadstone with her knowledge of the world, her wealth and many friends should live there. He wondered, too, what sort of a girl Miss Treadstone— the Miss Rosamond of whom the landlady had spoken—could be to shut herself up voluntarily in such seclusion.

But they were rowing in real earnest. Garth had made up his mind to get round a rock which formed the northern extremity of the little bay, and, though the tide was with them, Sir Oswald was aware that the under current was stronger than he had expected.

They had nearly reached the desired point when they became conscious that the sky, so clear and blue when they started, had suddenly clouded over. There were great dark banks of clouds on the horizon and the wind was rising until it threatened to become a hurricane. Evidently one of the storms of which the fisherman had spoken was upon them. Garth welcomed its coming with enthusiasm.

"Here is a chance to show what we can do," he cried as they turned and the boat sprang forward beneath their hands like a living thing.

Sir Oswald did not answer. He bent to his oars with renewed energy. The tide was on the turn, the wind was catching them sideways. It seemed to him that they would need all their skill to bring them back to Porthcawel in safety. They were nearing the Rock when they found themselves caught in one of the hidden currents of which they had been warned. Now, with the raging wind and turning tide, what was always a dangerous bit of water even to the experienced became a veritable maelstrom to Sir Oswald and Garth. In vain they put forth all their strength, their skiff was little more than a cockle-shell in the grasp of the element. At last a great wave catching them broadside turned the boat over and both men found themselves in the water.

Sir Oswald struck out blindly. He was not much of a swimmer at the best of times, and during this long period of blindness his muscles had got out of condition, so that he was in no state to fight the waves. He battled on, however, thinking of Maisie and his mother and Elizabeth. He was conscious that Garth was shouting encouragement, other noises seemed to mingle with the dash of the waves and the roar of the wind, then the darkness closed in upon him and for a time he knew no more.

He seemed to have been unconscious an eternity, when a glimmering of light returned to him. He became aware that he was being moved—carried—that he was on land, no longer buffeting with the waters. He heard voices that seemed very far off, Garth's and another, very soft and sweet, that he would have known among a thousand—Elizabeth's. For a minute he thought that death had passed, that he was already in Paradise, and he was content to rest in dreamy semi-consciousness.

Then some thought of what was being said penetrated to his brain.

"I believe his eyelids flickered," Garth was saying.

"Yes, I am sure I saw a movement," the other voice said, the one to which Sir Oswald often had listened in his blindness.

So she was alive then! This was no shadow land, but blessed flesh and blood reality. He tried to speak.

"Elizabeth! Elizabeth!" His weak lips strove to form the name he loved. With a supreme effort he opened his eyes to gaze upwards into the loveliest face he thought he had ever seen—a woman's face of purest oval, framed in masses of red-gold hair, with great, grey eyes that met his fully.

But Sir Oswald tried to look beyond for the face he wanted to see.

"Elizabeth! I want Elizabeth!" he said faintly, ere his head sank back and once more the darkness engulfed him.

Chapter Eighteen

SIR OSWALD was vaguely aware, through the thick mist that enveloped him, that he was being pommelled and rubbed, that his tongue and throat were hot and aching intolerably. Vaguely he saw always two faces—his cousin Garth's and that of an older man; he was conscious of only one desire, that they would let him relapse into the friendly darkness that seemed to be waiting for him. But the pommelling went on, and presently there was an exclamation of relief and some hot fluid poured down his throat. It brought the tears to his eyes, it made him cough and choke like a child.

Garth's voice said, "That's right, old fellow, now you'll do." And he was made to swallow a few more drops of the stimulant.

Then Sir Oswald opened his eyes and looked round. He saw that he was in a big bedroom, every features of which was unfamiliar to him; that beside Garth and the man he had seen before, a pleasant-faced, elderly woman was standing near the fire, apparently stirring some compound in a saucepan.

"Where am I?" he questioned, and his voice sounded very weak and far away.

The strange man took the answer upon himself.

"You are in Porthcawel Hold, my dear sir, and you have had just about as near a squeak for your life as any man ever did. That I can tell you."

"Who are you?" Sir Oswald asked feebly. He was beginning to realize that he was wrapped in blankets and that he was in a most disagreeable state of perspiration.

"I am John Spencer, at your service," the man said with a twinkle of his eye. "And I doctor the bodies of the people of Porthcawel, and many of them as can be got to be ill, that is to say, for it is a remarkably healthy place, and if it wasn't for a bit of a wreck now and then it is little enough I would have to do to keep my hand in. I had just come over to the Hold to have a talk to Lady Treadstone before the storm burst, and I am right glad I was here, as it enabled me to be of some use to you."

But Sir Oswald's attention had wandered. He looked at Garth. "Where is Elizabeth?"

"Elizabeth!" Young Davenant repeated in a puzzled tone. "Who is Elizabeth? Oh, you are dreaming, old chap. Nobody else has been here."

"Not here," Sir Oswald said weakly. "But when they were carrying me I heard her speaking."

Garth laughed. "Oh, my dear fellow, there was no one there but the men of the lifeboat who saved us, and Miss Treadstone."

"Miss Treadstone?" Sir Oswald repeated in a puzzled tone. "What is she like?"

"The most beautiful woman I ever saw in my life," Garth answered with enthusiasm. "Red-gold hair, grey eyes and a complexion like milk and roses.

Dr. Spencer laughed. "Ay, you are not the first that has called our Miss Rosamond Treadstone beautiful," he said dryly. "But now my patient has just got to go to sleep and think of nothing else, so I am going to turn you out of the room, Mr. Garth. Now, Sir Oswald, you will drink this." He held a cup to Sir Oswald's lips.

The other paused a moment before he drank.

"When are you going to get us back to the inn, doctor? We can't trespass on Lady Treadstone's hospitality."

"Well, we can none of us get to Porthcawel to-night, in the face of the storm," the doctor remarked philosophically. "And you have had a crack on your knee that will keep you a day or two longer than that, I'm thinking. But we shall know more about that to-morrow. For the present, all you have to do is just to drink this."

Sir Oswald obeyed mechanically. Every coherent thought of which he was conscious was centred on Elizabeth. That she was near him he felt certain. In the morning, when he was well, he would find her, his long search would be over. He soon fell into a profound sleep, one that lasted many hours. When next he opened his eyes the sunlight was streaming in through the open window, no trace of last night's storm was visible. As he lay on his pillows he could look across the blue water, scarcely stirred by a ripple, to the many coloured roofs of Porthcawel.

He felt very stiff as he tried to move, his right leg was numb and helpless. He had an early visit from Dr. Spencer, who assured him that his worst injury was a sprained knee, which would keep him a prisoner for a day or two.

"Anyhow, you would have had to have stayed," the doctor finished. "Lady Treadstone is too anxious to renew her acquaintance with you to let you go sooner. And as soon as you have had your breakfast, Mr. Garth and I are going to carry you into the morning-room, and then I warrant you won't find the time long."

Sir Oswald made no objection to this scheme. His one desire was to get downstairs to try and find Elizabeth.

Yet when he was established on the comfortable sofa in the morning-room he seemed as far from accomplishing his object as ever. Lady Treadstone came to him at once, the same pleasant, sweet-faced woman as ever, yet, as it struck him, with a new look—one which he would have described as a nervous, haunted look—in her eyes.

She greeted him warmly, and told him laughingly that she was glad of the wreck since it brought him to her doors.

Sir Oswald thanked her for all her kindness, but, when she went on to ask him about Maisie and his mother and her old friends at Davenant, it was easy to see that his attention was wandering and when she paused he broke in eagerly:

"Lady Treadstone, do you know where she is? You must, for I heard her talking as they brought me here. And you were always kind to her. I see now that you must have helped her. You will let me see her, won't you?"

Lady Treadstone looked at him apparently in absolute bewilderment. "Who are you talking about, Sir Oswald? I can't understand," she said.

"Why, of Elizabeth," Sir Oswald said quickly. "Elizabeth Martin. You always liked her."

"Oh! Of course," Lady Treadstone raised her eyebrows. "You mean Miss Martin, Maisie's governess. But what makes you come to me for information about her? I assure you there is no one at the Hold but my daughter and myself and the servants, and certainly Miss Martin is not one of them."

"But you know where she is—you can tell me where to find her?" Sir Oswald urged.

Lady Treadstone shook her head.

"Indeed I cannot," she said in a tone of finality. "She was not very amiable when I made some advances to her, Sir Oswald, and she left the Priory under such unpleasant circumstances that really"—she spread out her hands—"I quite wonder you should wish to find her," she added.

Sir Oswald raised his head, his face grew stem and serious. "Before you say any more, Lady Treadstone, may I tell you that my one great object in life is to find Miss Martin, to ask her to let me give her the shelter of my name—to make her my wife?"

"Sir Oswald!" Lady Treadstone's face expressed nothing but the profoundest amazement. "I am sorry I am quite unable to help you," she finished with a slight shrug of her shoulders. "Ah, here is Rosamond," as some one came along the terrace and paused before the open window. "Come in my dear. Here is Sir Oswald, not much the worse for last night's adventure after all."

Rosamond Treadstone stepped through the window. Sir Oswald knew at once that it was her face he had seen when he woke from unconsciousness. But it was the face of a woman, not a girl, and the grey eyes looked weary and sad.

She smiled, though, as she greeted Sir Oswald.

"I am so glad matters were no worse," she said quietly. "And see, I have brought you some daffodils. They are the first on the Rock, though they are blooming bravely in Porthcawel. I will put them in this jar, and then you can look at them." She turned to the table and stood at the near end of the sofa.

At her first words Sir Oswald started violently, then he lay still and looked at her. Surely Rosamond Treadstone was speaking with Elizabeth's voice. It sounded the same, and yet, as she went on, not quite the same. There was a certain quality in it that Elizabeth's had lacked, an added note of richness. But the likeness was there, it was unmistakable.

Lady Treadstone looked from one to the other with a smile.

"Well, now I think I will leave you two to become better acquainted," she said lightly. "I know Dr. Spencer has ever so many instructions to give me. I shall see you again presently, Sir Oswald. Mind you look after the invalid, Rosamond!" She nodded laughingly as she left the room.

Miss Treadstone went on talking as she arranged her flowers in a big Persian jar. If the white fingers were trembling as they moved among the daffodils, Sir Oswald saw nothing of it.

He watched the way the wonderful hair waved about her small head, the tiny little tendrils that curled round her temples, and all the while he was thinking not of Rosamond Treadstone's great beauty, but of the pale, quiet woman with the dark hair and the brown eyes whom he had pictured in his blindness at the Priory. At last he spoke abruptly:

"Miss Treadstone, was it your voice I heard when they were carrying me up from the beach?"

Miss Treadstone looked surprised. "Why, I suppose so," she said hesitatingly. "That is, if you really heard anyone's. You appeared to be unconscious."

"I heard a voice that I thought I recognized," Sir Oswald went on slowly. "But yours reminds me of it so strongly that I think I must have been mistaken."

Rosamond arched her brows. "Mine is the Treadstone voice. Perhaps you know my cousin, Lady Ermine Rivers. She has it too."

"No, I don't!" Sir Oswald said bluntly. "The owner of the voice I am thinking of is poor and friendless, working for her living. Yet the likeness is extraordinary."

"What is this friendless woman's name?" Miss Treadstone's voice was slightly sarcastic.

"Martin!" Sir Oswald answered. "Elizabeth Martin."

Miss Treadstone left her daffodils and sat down opposite.

"What was she like? Did she resemble me in appearance as well as in voice?"

"I—don't think so," Sir Oswald said uncertainly. "That is to say, I was blind. I never saw her face. But she has been described to me as pale and dark and tall. I believe she wore glasses."

"Um! Not a very attractive description," Miss Treadstone answered. "I'm afraid I can't help you, Sir Oswald. I am sure there is no one answering to it on the Rock. And a good many voices are similar in some respects."

"I have never heard anyone's that reminded me of hers but yours," Sir Oswald said decidedly.

Miss Treadstone got up quickly. "I don't know that I feel flattered," she said with a little shrug of her shoulders. "Now, Sir Oswald, I am going to pick you some more daffodils over there on the Rock." She stepped out through the window.

Left alone, Sir Oswald lay back on his couch feeling strangely puzzled. Some sixth sense told him that Elizabeth was near, and yet how was he to find her? He felt convinced that both Lady Treadstone and Rosamond could have told him more if they would. Both of them had impressed him as playing a part. But the more he thought of it the more certain he became that the key to Elizabeth's disappearance must lie within the Hold.

Rosamond Treadstone, too, had raised his interest in no ordinary degree. Even apart from the strange likeness her voice bore to the missing Elizabeth, her beauty, some touch of mystery there was about her, appealed to him strongly. He found himself picturing her face, trying to recall her faint, elusive smile.

Still his enforced inaction made the day seem a long one. Garth motored over to Poltrowen, a town where they had thought of staying for a day or two, and where letters might reasonably be expected to be awaiting them.

He got back just before dusk. There was a pile of correspondence for Sir Oswald, topped by one of Maisie's childish epistles. Garth left his cousin alone to get through it.

Sir Oswald was still smiling over some of Maisie's expressions when Rosamond Treadstone came softly into the room.

"I thought perhaps you might like to see the papers, Sir Oswald. They are late to-day. Oh, I beg your pardon."

She was turning away when Sir Oswald put out his hand.

"Please don't go," he said courteously. "This is a letter from my little girl, and she's rather quaint sometimes."

"Your little Maisie. I have heard my mother speak of her," Miss Treadstone said quietly. She seated herself in a low chair opposite. "How is she, Sir Oswald?"

"Quite well, thanks," he answered absently. "Poor little soul, she says she thinks she would rather have a blind daddy at home than a daddy with eyes who is always away."

Rosamond laughed. "Poor child! Well, I expect there is something to be said for her point of view."

"'And I wish my dear Miss Martin were back,'" Sir Oswald went on reading from the letter. "'Miss King is very good, but she doesn't tell me fairy tales, and she has headaches and can't play with me, and I heard her tell somebody the other day that I was a troublesome child.'"

"What a shame!" Miss Treadstone said indignantly. "Why, Maisie is the best child in the world if she is only managed properly. She—" She pulled herself up sharply.

But Sir Oswald had sprung up on his couch, his eyes ablaze with excitement. Forgetful of his sprained knee he stepped across the rug, he gripped her hands in his.

"How is it you know so much about Maisie?" he questioned fiercely. "You—because I know it now—because my heart told me, the first moment I heard your voice—because you are Elizabeth."

Chapter Nineteen

"You are Elizabeth!" Sir Oswald repeated. All the room seemed whirling round him with the shock of his discovery. Rosamond turned her face away, but he had seen the colour that surged over her cheeks in one hot, tumultuous flood that died away to pallor. She tried to free herself, but his hand held hers like a vice.

"Elizabeth! Why have you been so cruel to me—to all of us who cared for you? Why didn't you at least let us know that you were safe?"

Still the girl did not speak, her lips quivered faintly, but no sound came.

"You don't know how I have searched for you—how the fear that some evil had befallen you has haunted me by night and day."

His clasp was insensibly slackening, the pain in the bruised tendons of his knee was beginning to reassert itself.

She tore herself away. With a supreme effort she steadied her voice.

"You are making some strange mistake, Sir Oswald," she began. Then she caught sight of his face. "Your knee," she cried. "Dr. Spencer said it would not be fit to stand upon for a week yet and here you are—" She drew the sofa forward. "Sit down at once," she commanded.

The pain was making Sir Oswald dizzy, great beads of perspiration were standing on his brow, but he held out bravely.

"Not until you promise that you will not go away, that you will stay and tell me."

"Oh, but you are taking a mean advantage," the girl broke in passionately. "I will not—yes, yes!" as his face grew suddenly pale beneath its tan. "I will promise you anything you like, only sit down."

With a sigh of relief Sir Oswald sank back.

"Sit near me," he pleaded. "I want to see you. I want to realize what you are like, you wonderful new Elizabeth."

Rosamond did not obey, she stood on the rug, one hand lying on the high, carved mantelboard.

"Don't you think you take things a little too much for granted, Sir Oswald?" she questioned.

"No, I do not," he returned bluntly. "Do you think you could cheat me now? That you could make me believe that you are some one else, and not my Elizabeth at all? Can't you guess something of the joy it is to have found you—to know at least that you are safe? Ah, what torments I have gone through! Blind, helpless, unable even to defend you, dreading what a day might bring forth—" he broke off suddenly. "It won't bear thinking of. And all the while you were here, safe and well. If you had only sent us one word."

The woman standing before him drooped her head.

"I did not think you would care."

"You did not think I would care!" Sir Oswald repeated. "I had told you I loved you. I had asked you to be my wife."

"Yes." She stirred restlessly. She looked away from him down into the blazing heart of the fire. "But that was before you knew."

"Before I knew—what?" Sir Oswald questioned blankly.

"That I had come to your house under false pretences, that people called me a murderess," Rosamond said quietly enough, though her eyes were full of passionate misery.

"A murderess!" Sir Oswald repeated scornfully. "You—a murderess!" He laughed aloud at the very idea. "To think they should dare to bring such a charge against you. I would have thrown it back in their teeth. Had you come to me for help that night instead of going to Lady Treadstone, I would have advised you to face it out. I would have stood by your side through the world. Surely you did not doubt that we who knew you would be convinced that you were innocent?"

"No, I didn't know," Rosamond said wearily. All her strength seemed to desert her, she sat down suddenly in a chair at the end of the couch. "I couldn't expect you to believe my word—just my bare word," she went on, a growing passion in her voice. "I had deceived you. I had made my way into your house in my dead friend's name. I knew I could teach a little child like Maisie. It was only gradually afterwards that I came to see how wrong I had been."

"Wrong!" Sir Oswald cried. "You were not wrong, Elizabeth. You were most divinely right. We loved you, Maisie and I; what did it matter by what name you choose to be known? You were yourself, that was all that mattered."

"Yet the world is not generally so charitable to a woman who gets a situation through false references," Rosamond said calmly. "Oh, I assure you, Sir Oswald, I know every hard word that can be applied to my conduct—"

"Hard words, hard words!" Sir Oswald broke in hotly. "What do I care about them? All I can think of now is that all these weary months are over, that I have found you at last. Won't you give me at least a welcome, Elizabeth? Won't you tell me you are glad to see me?"

"What if I am not glad?" Rosamond asked passionately. "I have tried so hard to forget," she went on, with a quiver in her voice. "I have tried to put all the past from me and to live only in the present. And now you are bringing it all back to me—the misery and the pain and the humiliation—"

"Stop," Sir Oswald interrupted. His expression had grown suddenly colder. "Heaven knows I don't want to remind you of anything you wish to forget. If you bid me I will go out of your life altogether. You shall never hear of me again—if you tell me that you do not care for me, that there is no hope for me."

Rosamond did not speak. She looked away from him. Sir Oswald, leaning forward eagerly, could see only her delicate pro-file silhouetted against the carved oak wainscoting, the droop of her long upcurled lashes as they lay like a dark shadow upon the fairness of her skin. But something in her attitude, in the quiver of her lips, in some vague fashion gave him hope. He managed to catch one of the hands hanging listlessly at her side.

"What am I to do?"

"It would be much better for you if you did go away," she said beneath her breath.

"But do you want me to go?" Sir Oswald persisted. A new light was dawning in his eyes, his clasp was growing firmer. "Tell me, Elizabeth."

"I—don't know," she whispered.

"Don't you?" Sir Oswald drew her nearer. "You will have to let me help you to make up your mind, dear. Let me teach you to say two little words—'Stay, Oswald.'"

The girl caught her breath, once she tried to drag her hands from his. "Oh, I can't! And what is the good of it all? You can never be anything to me."

"Why not?" Sir Oswald questioned. "If we care for one another, that is all that matters."

"That is nothing," she contradicted. "The barrier between us can never be broken."

"What barrier?" Sir Oswald questioned, his face growing graver as he noted her agitation.

"The mystery of John Winter's death," she answered. "That must set me apart for ever."

"Not from the man who loves you," Sir Oswald said steadily. "Not from the man you love. Dear, give me the right to fight for you, let me make you my wife, and we will go abroad together while the cleverest detectives in Europe find out the truth."

For a moment the flush in Rosamond's face grew deeper, then it died away and left her very white. She put out her hand as though to thrust the very idea from her.

"No, no! I have told you it is impossible. Love and marriage are not for me. And you must go away and forget. Try and think how little you really know of me, and it will not be difficult."

"Won't it?" Sir Oswald laughed bitterly. "As for really knowing you, those months at the Priory last year, when you were an angel of pity to me in my blindness, were worth a life-time of ordinary acquaintanceship. Can't you trust me as you have trusted Lady Treadstone?"

"Trusted Lady Treadstone?" echoed Rosamond. "But don't you understand that she has cared for me for my dead father's sake, because she would not have disgrace brought on his name? If she has pitied me, if she has been kind as any mother to me, it has all been for my father's sake?"

Sir Oswald looked a little bewildered. The truth had not yet dawned on him.

"Your father?" he questioned. "Do you mean that he—?"

"My father was Lord Treadstone—Lady Treadstone's husband," Rosamond told him quietly. "She is my stepmother. It was on my account that she came down to the Priory and took Walton Grange, and when arrest seemed imminent, and I could think of no one else who could help me, I went to her."

"You are Lord Treadstone's daughter," Sir Oswald said slowly. "Then how or why did you—?"

"Did I marry John Winter, that is what you would ask me, isn't it?" she finished, drawing her hand from his. "By the maddest act of folly of which any girl was ever guilty. Oh, yes! You shall know the whole truth now. I was not quite seventeen, a spoiled, indulged only daughter, who had had her own way in everything. One day my father had been at home as affectionate as ever, the next I had a letter from him to tell me that he was to be married that very morning to a woman I had never even heard of. I went mad. I must have gone, really mad. I heard some of the servants talking, they were saying that it was partly on Miss Treadstone's account that my father had done it—that I wanted breaking in. It added fuel to my wrath, if any was needed. I rushed out and while I was still wild with rage I met John Winter."

She got up suddenly, and going over to the mantelpiece leaned her head on her hands.

A great pity dawned in Sir Oswald's eyes as he looked at her.

"Yes," he said slowly. "And he—?"

"He rented some land from my father and he trained horses and sold them," she went on in a low voice. "Latterly he had been breaking in a colt for us, and I—I knew every animal in the place; I had been down to see it several times and consequently had seen John Winter. I rather liked him; he was willing and agreeable, good-looking too, in a flashy kind of way. That afternoon he was on his way to the house to ask me to come down and look at the colt in harness in the new dog-cart. I—oh, how can I tell you what a fool I was?" She broke off, bitter scorn in her voice.

The pity in Sir Oswald's eyes grew and strengthened.

"I think I understand," he said quietly.

"How can you when I cannot even understand myself?" the girl questioned hotly. "He saw the tear-marks on my face, he saw the state of agitation I was in, and with a few adroit words he got the whole story out of me. Then he played upon my feelings until I burst out passionately that I would do anything to revenge myself upon my father. That I too would marry—would marry anybody. That was his opportunity, and he took it. The end of it was that I never went back to the house, that I went away with him to London. There he procured a special licence—he had saved a hundred or two, and was not inclined to spare them when it was a question of marrying Lord Treadstone's daughter—and before I had time to realize anything I was married."

She paused and glanced around. Sir Oswald caught a glimpse of the anguish in her eyes.

"That I awoke to find myself in hell was a foregone conclusion," she went on. "But I had a proud and stubborn nature. I hugged my poor revenge, I would not go to my father for help, and he would do nothing for me as long as I remained with my husband. That he—John—was disappointed is easily understood, and also that he vented his disappointment on me. The rest you can guess for yourself—the utter misery such folly must entail, culminating in that tragedy at Carlyn." She shuddered and hid her face in her hands.

Sir Oswald's knee was again forgotten as he stood up beside her.

"I can imagine everything," he said gravely. "But I want you to forget all that, dear. I want you to remember only that we are together and that we love each other."

For a moment he thought she was about to yield to his embrace, but she put out her hands to keep him at arm's length.

"I have never said I loved you."

"No you have not," he assented. "But you are going to, aren't you, Elizabeth? You don't know how I am longing to hear those words from your lips—'I love you, Oswald.'"

"Oh, what does it matter whether I do or don't?" she burst out passionately. "Because it must end here. What difference does it make?"

"All the difference in the world to me," Sir Oswald said as he drew her into his arms at last. "Just all the difference, my sweet Elizabeth. For you may be Rosamond to all the world. You will always be Elizabeth to me."

Chapter Twenty

Sir Oswald Davenant was resting after dinner. In accordance with Dr. Spencer's instructions it had been brought to him in the morning-room. Garth was dining with the Treadstones. Every now and then, when the dining-room door was opened, Sir Oswald could catch the sound of voices. He strained his ears and listened for the faintest echo of the one he loved. But it was always Garth who was talking, no slightest sound from Elizabeth reached him.

Presently, however, he could tell that they were leaving the dining-room. His face brightened, the expectancy in his eyes deepened. Surely she would have pity on him—his lady of delight. She had torn herself from him so abruptly an hour ago, she had refused to listen to him any longer, but she must know that he longed for her presence, how the very thought that she was in the house was a sort of intoxication to him. At last the door opened slowly, and Sir Oswald started forward eagerly, only to fall back with a sigh of disappointment when Lady Treadstone entered.

She smiled as she saw his expression. "I feel that I must apologize to you for being myself," she said as she sat down in a low chair by the fire. "But Rosamond has asked me to talk to you, Sir Oswald, to explain."

Sir Oswald stirred restlessly.

"It seems to me that we have had enough explanations. I don't want them, but I did want Elizabeth."

"But I am sure you will not refuse to hear what she wishes you to know?" Lady Treadstone returned with a quiet air of dignity.

She made a very gracious and pleasant picture as she sat there, the silk folds of her gown falling round her, priceless old lace shrouding her neck and wrists, the firelight shining on the jewels in her hair, gleaming round her throat and arms. But there was sadness in her smile and in the glance of her eyes.

"First she sends you a message," she went on slowly. "She bade me tell you that though you surprised the secret of her love from her this afternoon, you must forget it and her."

"Forget it and her!" Sir Oswald repeated incredulously. His dark face looked haggard as he leaned forward, his eyes were restless and eager.

"Tell her that I shall think of it and her every moment of my life," he said passionately. "What does she take me for? That she thinks I can forget at a word."

"She thinks you are her very true and loyal friend," said Lady Treadstone softly. "For anything else"—she spread out her hands—"she looks upon herself as one set apart, no closer ties are possible."

"They are possible. They shall be possible," affirmed Sir Oswald stoutly. He caught his breath quickly. "Won't you be on my side, Lady Treadstone? Can't you help me to persuade her to be my wife? To give me the right to defend her?"

Lady Treadstone looked back at him steadily.

"I am sure that I could not shake her determination, Sir Oswald, nor do I wish to. I believe her to be quite right. How could she marry you, or anyone, knowing that this charge of murder was hanging over her, that at any moment she might be arrested?"

That for one second before he answered Sir Oswald hesitated was obvious, and Lady Treadstone smiled slightly. He recovered himself instantly.

"I would take her abroad where no rascally detectives could find her," he said stoutly. "I will take care of her."

Lady Treadstone sighed.

"And what sort of a life would you lead, Sir Oswald? Haunted, a prey to a thousand fears. And what of your duties at the Priory, your mother and Maisie? No, Rosamond is right, she can never be your wife unless—"

Sir Oswald caught at the words. "Unless what?" he questioned eagerly.

"Unless the cloud is cleared away from her life," Lady Treadstone said impressively. "Until the world knows that she had no share in her husband's death, and the real murderer is found. Ah, Sir Oswald, it is a harder task than was ever set to knight-errant of old, but if you could do that—" she paused expressively.

Sir Oswald started.

"You have given me hope at last, Lady Treadstone," he cried enthusiastically. "I will devote my life to clearing her name, and then—then I will come back to the Hold."

"And I don't think you will come in vain," Lady Treadstone said soberly. "But there is much to do before that can happen, Sir Oswald." She put up her handkerchief and wiped away a tear. "You don't know how I have longed for someone to give me help and counsel," she went on. "The whole story seems fraught with mystery. Often I lie awake all night thinking of it, trying to see some explanation. My poor Rosamond cannot bear to speak of Winter's death. Until last night I had never heard from her the true story of that dreadful day as she knew it."

Sir Oswald sat upright, a look of energy and purpose had come into his face, and his eyes were bright and determined.

"Please give me all the help you can, Lady Treadstone. Tell me everything you know."

"I will, very gladly," was Lady Treadstone's response.

She leaned back in her chair and holding up her fan moved it to and fro in her delicate fingers as she spoke.

"Rosamond has told you the story of her most unhappy marriage, I know," she said slowly. "I will leave that, except to say that I shall always blame myself for my share in it, for consenting to marry Lord Treadstone, the lover of my girlish days, without insisting on making his daughter's acquaintance first. He thought it best so, the girl had been so spoiled, she would resent the marriage less if she knew nothing of it until it was an accomplished fact. The event proved how utterly he was wrong, and Rosamond in her anger spoiled her own life and broke her father's heart. For he was never the same afterwards; he had been very proud of her beauty and high-spiritedness, and the news of her elopement was the most horrible blow to him. As for her, poor unhappy girl, one can imagine what her life must have been with a man like Winter—a man, moreover, who cared nothing for her, who only thought of marrying Lord Treadstone's heiress."

She stopped a moment and looked into the flames with reflective eyes.

Sir Oswald did not speak, but the lines of his mouth were stern beneath his drooping dark moustache; his right hand clenched and unclenched itself nervously.

Presently Lady Treadstone went on:

"Winter soon found that he had made a mistake. Rosamond had no money of her own; there had been some flaw in her mother's marriage settlement, and her father refused to help her while she remained with her husband, and unhappy as she was the girl was far too proud to confess her mistake. Winter lost money over his farming, over his attempt at horse training, drifted from one thing to another until finally he became gamekeeper at Carlyn Hall. Then the final tragedy began. Rosamond had had one child; it died the year before they went to Carlyn, and she was more miserable and more embittered than ever. She had no friends, and it was impossible for her to associate intimately with the village women. Then Frank Carlyn came to the cottage one day. He was kind and sympathetic; he spoke to her as if she had been of his own class, he offered to lend her books. He came again and talked them over with her. Rosamond has told me, and I fully believe her, that there was nothing, not even friendship between them; but his visits to the cottage were noticed, and comments upon them reached Winter's ears. He was furious; coming home the worse for drink, he abused Rosamond in the coarsest terms; from words he went on to blows."

Sir Oswald drew a long breath.

"Brute! I wish I had had the good luck to be the man that shot him."

"Ah!" He could see that Lady Treads tone was deeply moved, her voice trembled as she went on. "In the midst of it Frank Carlyn appeared on the scene; he, of course, espoused Rosamond's part, and further infuriated Winter, who assailed him with the vilest accusations and threats. The quarrel was hot and furious; terrified, Rosamond rushed away into the wood; how long she remained there, crouching and sobbing, she never knew, but when at last she made her way back to the cottage all was quiet—too quiet. Of Carlyn there was no sign, but Winter lay in front of the cottage dead. Then Rosamond made the second great mistake of her life. She felt convinced that Carlyn had killed her husband; she knew that if she stayed to face the inevitable inquiry the fact that she was Lord Treadstone's daughter was certain to leak out. It never occurred to her that she might be accused of the murder, and she thought that by running away she would avoid bringing this terrible disgrace upon the father she still loved. She had always kept up with one friend of her past life, Elizabeth Martin, the vicar's daughter, and in her despair she turned to her for refuge. Miss Martin was just then living in rooms in London; she took Rosamond in and mothered her; she tried to persuade her to declare herself. In vain; Rosamond was terrified when she found herself accused of the murder in the papers, and nothing could be done with her. When illness overtook Miss Martin she had just obtained the post of governess to Maisie, and on her death-bed the scheme whereby Rosamond took her place was evolved by her. The rest you know, Sir Oswald."

"Some of it!" Sir Oswald qualified. His deep-set eyes were bright and eager. "But there is one important point that I want clearing up. Who do you, who does Rosamond, think killed her husband?" Lady Treadstone sighed again.

"Rosamond has never doubted that Frank Carlyn fired the fatal shot in a rage," she said slowly. "And she blames herself cruelly for her share in the matter, for her folly, as she calls it, in talking to Carlyn and reading his books, and thereby rousing Winter's anger."

Sir Oswald leaned back in his chair.

"Frank Carlyn never did it," he said conclusively. "Though I haven't seen much of him of late years I knew him well as a boy; he was frank, generous and open-hearted, passionate too, I grant. He might have shot Winter in a rage. But as for concealing the fact and letting a woman be accused of his crime and hunted high and low—why, the idea is impossible, unthinkable."

"So I have sometimes argued," Lady Treadstone assented, shutting up her fan and letting it drop in her lap. "But if he did not, who did? There does not seem to be room for a third person in Rosamond's story."

"Room or not, there is one," Sir Oswald declared vigorously; he paused a moment, then he broke out again energetically, "I'll go down to Carlyn at once. I have been told sometimes that I have the detective instinct. I'll see if I can't make use of it for once."

Lady Treadstone did not look very hopeful. It seemed to her that not much could be expected of amateur help. She would have preferred to hear that Sir Oswald was going to engage a capable private detective. Still, she did not argue; time, she reflected, would probably show him the wiser course.

She got up now and standing for a moment on the fur rug, looked down at the young man with her faint, troubled smile.

"I think your cousin wants to see you! I will send him in now that I have accomplished my errand. If I have somewhat exceeded my instructions—well, I hope I shall not find it difficult to win Rosamond's forgiveness."

Sir Oswald caught her hand as she passed and pressed his lips to it.

"You have at least gained my eternal gratitude," he said fervently. "You have given me something to hope and work for. I will find this cowardly scoundrel, Lady Treadstone."

"I hope so," she said wistfully, as she opened the door. She waited a minute, as if about to speak, then changing her mind she closed the door behind her. In the hall she hesitated; she could hear voices, Garth Davenant's and her step-daughter's.

In the clear light given off by the wax candles in their tall silver sconces, her face looked white and strangely troubled.

"The third person," she whispered to herself. "Yes, of course he must be found. There must have been one—of course, there must have been one—but I must not think of that, or I shall go mad."

Chapter Twenty-One

THE CARLYN ARMS was the best inn in Carlyn village. It was a quaint black and white timbered, many gabled building, but its interior looked homely and pleasant. Through the big bow window in the bar there was a wonderful view of the country with a glimpse of the blue outlines of the Welsh hills in the distance.

Sir Oswald Davenant, coming out of the station, found himself nearly opposite this attractive hostelry, and after a moment's hesitation he walked in.

He had come down to Carlyn in pursuit of his resolve to clear Rosamond Treadstone of any share in the murder of John Winter, but, born detective though he had called himself, now that he was actually on the spot he felt at a loss how to set about his work. Rosamond's story gave him no help, and for the first time, as he stood on the threshold of the "Carlyn Arms" and was confronted by a tall, young woman with a white face and tragic dark eyes, he felt inclined to despair.

He asked if he could have a room and lunch. Later on he was going to walk up to the Hall, but first he thought he would try whether it was possible to learn anything from local gossip.

At first it seemed unlikely that he would be successful. The young woman who waited upon him was singularly silent. She replied to his attempts at conversation in monosyllables, but with the advent of lunch the landlord arrived upon the scene and everything altered. He was only too anxious to talk to his customer, while the young woman busied herself among the glasses at the bar.

Sir Oswald began with the usual chat about the weather and the prospects of the crops, then by an easy transition he passed to the murder in the Home Wood.

The landlord pursed up his lips and shook his head.

"Ay, that was a bad job," he said solemnly. "A bad job."

"I suppose you knew them both?" Sir Oswald hazarded. "Winter and his wife, I mean."

"I knew Jack Winter well enough," the landlord assented. "He was here oftener than I wanted, or than was for his own good. But as for his wife, well, there was nobody about here that could be said to know her. As for me, I don't know that I ever set eyes on her. Now, Esther, my girl, there's plenty for you to do there."

But the dark-eyed, young woman had already vanished, and the door behind the bar was closed firmly.

There was a queer look in the landlord's eyes as he glanced after her.

"She can't stand any talk about the murder," he said with a nod of his head at the bar. "Always flies out when it is mentioned."

"Why should she do that?" Sir Oswald questioned without much interest.

The landlord winked as he removed one of the dishes.

"Well, I have my own notions as to that, sir. Esther Retford was the only woman about here that knew Mrs. Winter. Her brother, Jim Retford, was the one that found the body. It sent him into a fit and he has never been the same since, poor lad, always subject to these attacks he is, and they call him 'Softy Retford.' Esther would tell you that is what upsets her, but I have my own opinions."

"It is enough to make her fight shy of the subject though," Sir Oswald remarked. "But what is your theory, landlord?"

"Well, I don't know that I should go so far as to call it that, sir," the man said doubtfully. "But—well, there's a boy at Retford's cottage that is the very spit of Jack Winter. They give out that it is the child of a married sister come down for a change of air. All I know is that Jack Winter won't ever be dead while that child is alive."

Sir Oswald drew a deep breath. "Oh, that was it, was it? I didn't know Winter was that sort of a man."

"He was pretty much all sorts that was bad," the landlord returned emphatically. "A real rotten lot was Winter, sir. And it's often been in my mind that it was over Esther Retford, him and his wife quarrelled and she shot him; it would have all come out if there had been a trial, but now we shall never know."

Sir Oswald's face darkened. He hated to hear this careless talk of Rosamond. He hated to remember that she had ever been another man's wife, the very thought that she had belonged to a low common boor such as Winter was agony to him. Yet he knew that he must brace himself, must prepared to hear her discussed, criticized, blamed even, in silence, if by any means he was to help her.

Meanwhile the landlord went on with his story, pleased with the interest it was exciting:

"The day before the murder Esther Retford went away suddenly, ran away, folks called it, then there had been some talk about her and Winter in the village—none too kind talk—and folks put two and two together. Then some six months ago Esther came back, and a month or two after that they brought this boy to the cottage. Old Retford preached us a nice tale about him, but we are not quite blind at Carlyn."

"I am sure you are not," agreed Sir Oswald, who was not ignorant of village ways. "But how do you come to have the young woman here, landlord?"

"Well, my wife is ill, sir, and she always liked Esther, and we have to have help of some kind, and the wife she said it would give the girl a chance, and she is cheap, and it don't do for any of us to be reckoning up other folk's past mistakes," concluded the worthy man charitably.

Sir Oswald smiled a little as he got up, wondering whether charity or the fact that her services were cheap had most to do with procuring Esther Retford her situation. But her story, sordid and pitiful though it was, did not seem likely to help him much in his quest. He determined to walk up to the Hall and see whether he would be more successful with Frank Carlyn. He asked the way to the Home Wood, and set off at a brisk pace towards it catching one more glimpse of Esther Retford's white face as he left the inn.

It haunted his thoughts as he walked along. This was another ruined life to be laid to Winter's account. But as he entered the Home Wood he forgot everything but Rosamond; he pictured her moving about among its glades and mossy paths, a tall, gracious figure in her simple gowns with her crown of golden hair wound about her head.

Spring was later at Carlyn than at Porthcawel. The young larches in the Home Wood were just bursting into leaf, at their feet the wild hyacinths were fading away, mistily blue, while the rhododendrons and the gorse were in bud which later on would make the country-side one golden glory.

Sir Oswald came soon to the clearing in which the gamekeeper's cottage stood. He waited a moment and looked at it, its miniature gables and the creepers climbing its walls, and involuntarily he raised his hat and stood bareheaded. So it was here she had lived and suffered, the lady of his love. Here the martyrdom of her married life, the tragedy of its close, had been enacted.

It was evident that no one was living there now: the little garden was choked with weeds, long strands of ivy were drooping over the windows. The path where John Winter had lain dead was scarcely distinguishable from the tangled flowerbeds on either side. Sir Oswald gazed at it all as though he would wring the past secret from it.

Suddenly, as he waited, he heard a curious, strangled sound from among the bushes beside him; at first he thought it came from some animal in pain, but as it went on he became aware that it was distinctly human, a hoarse, persistent sobbing in which some distinguishable words seemed to mingle. It died away at last into a low moaning.

Sir Oswald stepped across quickly and parted the bushes. Something lay on the ground shaking and choking. At first it was difficult to distinguish anything, but as Sir Oswald's eyes grew clearer, he saw that it was a boy—a big, overgrown lad who crouched there in a forlorn, shapeless heap.

"What is the matter?" asked Sir Oswald gently.

The boy started violently, lay still for a minute, then slowly lifted a tear-stained, miserable face, and, after one stare at Sir Oswald, shambled to his feet and prepared to make off.

Sir Oswald caught his shoulder. "What is your name, lad? And what are you doing here?"

There was a series of wild jerks from side to side, and then the boy accepted capture.

"I come to look for feyther," he explained sullenly.

"And who is feyther?" Sir Oswald questioned further, with an authoritative shake.

"Retford, the keeper," the lad stammered. "Let me go, sir! He'll be looking for me. And it is a hiding I get if his dinner is late."

He swung up a tin from the ground as he spoke, and Sir Oswald slackened his hold on the boy's arm.

"And what were you howling in that fashion for, young Retford?"

The lad returned no answer; ducking his head he made a sudden bolt for liberty and reached the open.

Sir Oswald made no effort to recapture him. He walked on in the direction of Carlyn Hall, frowning as he walked. So this lad was Esther Retford's brother, the boy who had been the first to find John Winter's body, and who had had fits and been softy like ever since, as the landlord had said. What brought the lad back to the scene of his terrible discovery, and what memory accounted for his sobbing fit? Sir Oswald could not see clearly yet, but some instinct seemed to warn him that the first thread that was to lead to the undoing of the mystery of John Winter's death had been placed in his hands to-day.

He felt as if Fate and something stronger than Fate was on his side and Rosamond's at last.

As he came in sight of the wicket-gate leading into the park, Fortune favoured him once more. Frank Carlyn came across the grass, moving slowly, with his head bent as if in thought. He stared in amazement when he saw Sir Oswald.

"Why, Davenant, what lucky wind has blown you here?" he cried.

But it was noticeable that he did not hold out his hand and that Sir Oswald did not offer his or pass to Carlyn's side of the gate. Instead he leaned over the top bar.

"I came on purpose to see you, Carlyn. I heard you had returned from your big game expedition."

"Yes. We had bad luck there," Carlyn grumbled. "But why on earth didn't you let a fellow know you were coming, Davenant? And where is your luggage? Have you left it at the station?"

"My bag is at the 'Carlyn Arms,'" Sir Oswald said quietly. "I did not come to trespass on your hospitality, Carlyn. I want to claim your help."

"My help?" Carlyn raised his eyebrows. "In what way?" he questioned briefly.

Davenant looked him squarely in the eyes.

"I have come here to find the murderer of John Winter."

Carlyn's face became suddenly set like a mask.

"Why do you come to me for help?"

Sir Oswald's gaze did not relax.

"Because I believe that but for his murderer you were the last person to see John Winter alive."

Carlyn turned his head aside.

"Very possibly I might have been," he returned in a voice made intentionally indifferent. "I had just given the man notice. The coverts were in a disgraceful state, and when I spoke of it he was insolent."

"Quite possibly. But it was not about the coverts you quarrelled," Sir Oswald said in the same cool, level voice.

Carlyn swung round and faced him.

"What do you know about a quarrel? And what business is it of yours, anyhow? What have you to do with John Winter?"

"I have nothing whatever to do with John Winter," Sir Oswald said slowly. "But it is my business to inquire into his murder, because I mean to marry his widow."

Chapter Twenty-Two

THERE WAS a moment's tense silence, then Carlyn spoke in a harsh, changed voice: "I cannot help you in any way. I must ask you not to speak to me of the matter again." He turned on his heel.

Sir Oswald swung the gate aside and strode after him.

"Perhaps you will answer one question, Carlyn. Did you, in the heat of your quarrel, pick up John Winter's gun and, either by accident or intention, fire it at him?"

Carlyn's face was white with rage as he faced his interlocutor.

"Why don't you call me a murderer at once?" he demanded roughly. "But I will answer a fool according to his folly. I did not fire Winter's gun. I did not even see it. When I parted from him he was as well as you or I. Now are you satisfied?

"Not quite," Sir Oswald said quietly "How was it that you did not reassure Mrs. Winter as to your entire innocence in the matter when you met her in my house as Miss Martin?

Carlyn uttered a sharp, incredulous sound, then he stood still.

"I have said all I mean to say, Davenant. For anything else I must refer you to Mrs. Winter herself."

"Perhaps I can answer my question," Sir Oswald went on in a perfectly unmoved voice. "Because you believe that Mrs. Winter fired the fatal shot herself. Suppose I tell you that all along she has believed the same of you, and thought herself responsible only in so far as her friendship for you might have given Winter some cause for anger. It is to clear this matter up that I have come here, and I shall not rest until the real murderer is brought to justice."

Carlyn's face altered indefinably; there was something very like pity in his eyes as he looked at the other man.

"You will never do that, old chap. Let me advise you, go back to the Priory and forget all about John Winter's—death." He paused before the last word. It was obvious that he had been about to substitute another.

"I think not," Sir Oswald remarked, tightening his lips. "My present intention is to go back to the inn and to devote myself to going over all the details of the case. I shall want your help later, Carlyn, and I shall call upon you to give it. Just now I am going up to the rectory. I want to see Miss Burford. I am the bearer of various messages from—Elizabeth." He could not bear to think or speak of his lovely, dainty Elizabeth by the dead man's name, he had not yet accustomed himself to the new Rosamond.

"To Barbara!" Carlyn's tone was insensibly softened. "But why should Mrs. Winter send messages to Barbara?"

"Because Barbara helped her to escape from the Priory when the detectives were at her heels." Sir Oswald looked somewhat surprised in his turn. "Didn't you know? She helped her with the tenderest pity and womanly compassion. It would be impossible to tell you all we owe to Barbara Burford."

Frank Carlyn pushed his cap back from his brow, his eyes were full of bewilderment.

"Barbara helped her to escape!" he repeated. "But why should Barbara help her?"

There was a dawning smile in Sir Oswald's grey eyes as he looked at the young man's puzzled face.

"Do you know, Carlyn," he said very deliberately. "I think that is one of the questions you should put to Barbara herself."

He did not wait for any rejoinder. For the present he had learned all he had expected from Carlyn; the rest he must do for himself, though, as he had said, he might need the young man's help later on.

Carlyn stood looking after his retreating figure, his mind a whirl of perplexity. Barbara's rejection of him had gone deeper than he had thought at the time; she had been so intertwined with his life that he had not realized at first how dismal it would be without her. He had never been able to understand that sudden change in her, the apparent coldness that resulted from her visit to the Priory. Was it possible that Sir Oswald knew something that he did not? But puzzle over it as he might he was no nearer guessing the truth.

A strange restlessness possessed him. He could settle to nothing. Some friends from a neighbouring house drove over to tea and tennis, and he made a most unobservant, absent-minded host. He could not talk society platitudes while his mind was full of Barbara—Barbara, with her shy, sweet eyes, her slender, elusive grace. He had likened her sometimes during their brief engagement to an English rose, and it was as a rose he thought of her now, with her fair complexion, her crown of dusky hair, and the smile that came and went upon her lips and lay hidden in her eyes.

After dinner he strolled across the park with his cigar and the dog, Bruno. Insensibly his feet led him towards the village in the direction of the Rectory. As he neared the familiar gate he caught sight of a white dress in the garden and knew that Barbara, as was her custom, was walking up and down waiting for her father, who was probably dozing in the dining-room, but who liked to find her ready when he came out for a saunter round the garden in the twilight.

Carlyn stood looking at her silently, but his cigar would have betrayed his presence even if Bruno had not bounded forward with his welcome.

"Ah, Frank!" Barbara said quietly. "Somehow I thought you might walk over this evening. Sir Oswald Davenant is dining with us." Her eyes were troubled, her lips trembled as they shook hands.

"Oh, I didn't know," Carlyn said almost indifferently as he held her hand a minute. "Oh, yes, I remember. He said he had messages for you. Did he tell you his news?"

The sadness in Barbara's eyes deepened.

"Yes, he told me. I am so sorry, Frank."

"Well, every man must please himself," Carlyn observed philosophically. "You never told me that you engineered the escape from the Priory, Barbara."

Barbara was thankful that the gathering dusk hid the colour that leapt into her cheeks. "Oh, didn't I?" she said lamely.

"No." Carlyn looked down at her curiously. "You are a plucky little girl. But what put it into your head, Barbara?"

"I don't know," Barbara answered evasively. "I was sorry for her, of course."

"And now you are sorry Davenant is going to marry her," Carlyn said gravely. "Did you think she was guilty of the murder when you helped her?"

"I don't know," the girl murmured restlessly. "Oswald does not."

Carlyn laughed dryly. "Obviously he does not. He did me the honour to ask if I had been the murderer, just now."

"What—you?" Barbara said incredulously. "How dare he? He must be mad."

"Oh, I don't think so," Carlyn said generously. "Except on one point, perhaps. He told me to ask you why you helped Mrs. Winter to escape."

Barbara's face altered suddenly. "Oh, did he? I wonder what should make him do that?"

"So do I," Carlyn assented. "I have been puzzling about it ever since. Just now, when you said you were sorry to hear his news, a glimmering of an idea came to me. I suppose it wasn't right, Barbara?"

Barbara turned aside, and plucking a spray of sweet-scented syringa held it to her lips.

"I shouldn't think it was likely," she said unsteadily. "I believe I ought to go back now, Frank. Father is sure to want some music, as Sir Oswald is here."

"The idea came to me when I saw your eyes," Carlyn went on. "They seemed—they looked as if they were sorry for me."

"Oh, you can't tell anything by people's eyes," Barbara said, and her laugh had a touch of hysteria in its ring. "You mustn't be fanciful, Frank."

"I wish you were," Frank said gravely. "Because I have been very sorry for myself—ever since you threw me over, Barbara."

He caught the hand that still held the syringa and crushed it in his.

"Ah, Barbara, Barbara, you are a hard-hearted little girl. Won't you take pity on me again? I can't do without you. Your face haunted me day and night while I was away."

Barbara's hand lay quiescent in his now, the syringa dropped unheeded to the ground.

"But I thought you cared for someone else," she stammered.

Carlyn took both her hands now and held them tightly gripped in one of his.

"And I thought you didn't care for me," he whispered. "Oh, Barbara, hasn't it been just one big mistake, little girl?"

Barbara's brown head drooped very low.

"I think perhaps it has," she stammered with quivering lip.

Carlyn's arms found their way round her waist, her head was drawn upon his shoulder. "Sweetheart," he said passionately, as his lips sought hers, "this is the real thing, isn't it? That other last time was only make-believe. But you do care a little now, don't you?"

"Just a little," Barbara said in a trembling voice. "Oh, Frank, Frank, you silly boy, didn't you know I always cared?"

"Umph!" Carlyn said dryly, his eyes just a trifle misty. "How could I know? You took such a remarkably queer way of showing it, Miss Burford."

"Oh, Frank!" Barbara drew back and held him at arm's length, her hands resting on his breast. "I couldn't go on with it—our engagement—while—while I thought you liked her best."

"Liked who best?" Carlyn demanded. "Come, Barbara, I must know."

Barbara's eyelids sank.

"Why, her—Mrs. Winter," she replied. "People said you did, you know, Frank."

"And you believed them?" Carlyn said, giving her a fond, possessive shake. "Ah, you silly, silly little girl! Are you always going to believe everything you hear against me, Barbara?"

"No, no!" the girl whispered, clinging to him. "Never again, Frank."

Carlyn's eyes wandered proudly over the small flower-like head, the delicate, high-bred face.

"So you helped her to escape, though you thought I cared for her, but you could not stand me afterwards."

"Yes, yes," Barbara agreed feverishly. "Of course that was how it was. I knew her directly I saw her at the Priory."

"Did you?" A new light was dawning in Carlyn's eyes, his expression was very tender as he gazed downwards at the pretty, confused face. "And then you found out that the detectives had come to take her?"

"Yes." A tiny smile crept round Barbara's mouth. "I played the eavesdropper, Frank. I overheard a detective talking to Sybil Lorrimer and I listened."

Carlyn smiled too.

"A good thing for her you did. And you managed to circumvent them?"

"Yes," Barbara said with deepening colour. "At first I couldn't think of anything, then I remembered that Algy Turner was coming in his car, and everything was very easy. It was quite simple, really."

"Quite," Carlyn assented with a little twist of his mouth. "And you did all this, took all this responsibility upon yourself for the woman you thought I loved. Why did you do it, Barbara?"

"I told you," the girl began; then she lifted her eyes, and she met the look in his, she yielded herself in sudden soft surrender. "It was for your sake," she whispered. "Because I thought you loved her."

Carlyn's arm had stolen round her again, his head was very near hers. "Why did you do it for my sake, Barbara?"

Barbara turned her face away. "Because I—" Then gathering up her courage she lifted up her face bravely—"because I—any woman would do anything for the sake of the man she loved."

Chapter Twenty-Three

MR. GREGG stood in the door of the post office at Bathurat, the nearest town to Porthcawel, of which it was within an easy ride. The detective was looking down the street somewhat anxiously. Presently he saw the man for whom he was looking, and went to meet him.

Mr. Marlowe's usually satisfied face looked worried and anxious. "No luck again, sir."

Mr. Gregg took his arm. "Hush, Marlowe! Remember any passer-by may know the secret that is puzzling us. I always try to think of that. Wait till you get to my room."

He led the way to a bright and spacious apartment, overlooking the street in the principal commercial hostelry of Bathurat. There he seated himself in a comfortable arm-chair and motioned Marlowe to the one opposite.

"Well, what now?"

Mr. Marlowe wiped his brow with a large handkerchief. "Of all the females I have ever met she is the most elusive!" he burst out. "Here have I been making inquiries of every one at Porthcawel, scraping acquaintance with the servants at the Hold, and all to no purpose. Not one word of her, or anyone like her, could I hear. Then yesterday, when I made up my mind we were on the wrong track altogether, suddenly I saw her, straight there before me."

"You saw her!" For once Mr. Gregg was stirred out of his habitual calm. "What did you do?"

Marlowe scratched his head sheepishly. "I let her give me the slip again, sir, that's what I did. I'll just tell you how it was. This last week or two I have got a bit friendly with one of the maids at the Hold, and though there didn't seem anything to be got out of her she had promised to come out for a chat with me yesterday afternoon. I was waiting for her, keeping myself out of sight among the rocks, for they don't welcome visitors at the Hold, when all of a sudden I heard a little noise behind me. I turned round, thinking that my friend had come, and there just behind me, as large as life stood Mrs. Winter."

He paused dramatically.

Mr. Gregg's face did not alter. "Well?"

The ex-constable looked a little disappointed. "I jumped up. I was sitting on a bit of stone, and there we stood staring at one another—the woman and me. She knew me too; I saw that in her eyes, and her face went very white, and she looked frightened to death. I was too taken aback with the suddenness of it all to move, and so I think was she. But at last she turned and ran back. I went after her as fast as I could. Right up against the Rock she went into a sort of cave. It was all dark inside, but I was gaining on her every instant. I could hear her deep breathing, I could almost catch her skirts when my feet gave way under me. I fell suddenly down, hitting my head as I went a nasty crack."

For the first time Mr. Gregg noticed that his subordinate's head was decorated with a strap of black plaster. "And when you got up?" he said interrogatively.

"She was gone," Marlowe said shamefacedly. "I was a bit dazed like for a minute. I had fallen down a couple of rough steps, but there wasn't a sight or sound of her anyways about. Got right away again she had."

"Umph!" Mr. Gregg tightened his lips and tapped reflectively on the open pages of his notebook with his pencil. "Sure you really saw her, are you, Marlowe?" he asked cynically. "You had not been partaking too freely of the home brewed at the inn, and then went to sleep on the stone, while you were waiting for your friend, and dreamt it all."

"Sir," protested the indignant Marlowe, "I hadn't touched a drop of anything. I saw her as plain as I ever saw anyone in my life. It wasn't possible that there could be any mistake."

Mr. Gregg did not speak for a minute, his bushy brows were drawn together from under them, his eyes gazed at Marlowe in a puzzled fashion.

"What did she look like? How was she dressed?" he asked.

"She was dressed in some rough stuff," Marlowe said sullenly, "and she wore a sort of hood over her head, same as I have seen her once or twice when I have met her about the woods at Carlyn. Well, as for looks she hadn't altered much, might be she was a bit fatter, and her hair was the same colour as it used to be, not dyed black like it was at the Priory."

"Same colour as it used to be, was it?" Mr. Gregg questioned slowly. He bit the top of his pencil meditatively. "So that is all you can tell me?"

Marlowe scraped his foot on the floor. "Yes, I think so. There was just one thing. The cave, as I thought it was, that she ran into, I have just found out is just a private way up to the Hold. In the old days they say it was used for smuggling."

Mr. Gregg got up and strolled to the window. "Well, at any rate you have proved that we were right in thinking she was at the Hold. I always felt sure that Lady Treadstone had something to do with it, and when Sir Oswald came down here I was more certain than ever. Even Inspector Church will be convinced now. There will be money in this for both of us, Marlowe."

The ex-constable's face looked grim. "It isn't the money I care about now, sir, though I thought of that at first, but it is the being outwitted by a woman. She had done nothing but make fools of us from first to last, sir."

"She won't make fools of us much longer," said Mr. Gregg quietly. "It has been a difficult case, but I think I see daylight at last. Miss Lorrimer put us in the way when she told us about Lady Treadstone taking a fancy to this Miss Martin and wanting her to go and see her, and yesterday I had a bit of luck. I found a man who had been working in the garden at Walton when Miss Martin disappeared from the Priory. He had been keeping company with the under housemaid, and that very night they were doing a bit of sweethearting in the dark, and at a side door, and to make a long story short they saw a woman in a dark dress of some kind come round the house and go to the morning-room, where Lady Treadstone was sitting."

Marlowe coughed impatiently. "Now why on earth couldn't they have told us this before? To think of the time and trouble it would have saved us."

Mr. Gregg shrugged his shoulders. "The bucolic mind works slowly. They strolled round after her, and were in time to hear the window of the morning-room shut, and the blind pulled down, but there was no sign of the lady, and they never heard any more of her. However, it just gives us the confirmation we wanted. Now we can set to work in real earnest. I have had a guard set at all the nearest stations, and the private landing-stage at the Hold is watched. I don't think she can escape us this time."

"I wouldn't answer for it," Marlowe said gloomily. "As slippery as an eel she is. I shan't ever feel sure of her till she is landed in gaol, if then."

The Winter affair had shaken the ex-constable's confidence in himself. He had been so sure that he had only wanted his opportunity to make his mark, and here he found himself circumvented at every turn by a woman. He felt inclined to throw the whole thing up in despair sometimes.

Mr. Gregg paced up and down the room restlessly. He was a little nearer the solution than Marlowe, but there was much that puzzled even him yet. "The question is, where has Lady Treadstone hidden her," he went on, coming to a standstill before his subordinate and eyeing him narrowly. "You are certain that she is not disguised as one of the servants at the Hold?"

"Quite certain!" Marlowe returned emphatically. "Naturally that was the first thing I thought of. But I have made it my business to see them all and there isn't one that resembles her. No, I can't make out where she is," he finished in a puzzled tone. "My friend, the housemaid, swears that there isn't a woman at the Hold but the servants and her ladyship and Miss Treadstone."

"Ay! Miss Treadstone," Gregory repeated thoughtfully. "Have you seen her, Marlowe?"

"No, I can't say that I have. But surely you would never think—"

"I get queer thoughts sometimes like other folks," Mr. Gregg returned philosophically. "Miss Treadstone was not at Walton?"

"No. But there can't be any mistake." Marlowe was perspiring freely in his excitement. "Lots of people at Porthcawel remember Miss Treadstone as a child. They call her Miss Rosamond."

"Oh, there is a Miss Treadstone safe enough," Mr. Gregg said at once. "I looked her up in the peerage. What has occurred to me is—is this the real Miss Treadstone at the Hold?"

"By Jove!" Marlowe exclaimed, then his face fell. "Oh, I don't think there is any mistake about that. She has been to see the landlady at the inn on the beach, who remembers her as a child and talks a lot about Miss Rosamond, and they had a long chat over old times. Mrs. Tregarth told me about it herself, and said the young lady was just like her mother."

Mr. Gregg pursed up his lips. "Umph! Well, that is another check. Still we can't help it. Now then, I want you to step over to the post office with me, Marlowe. It is the only place in this confounded town that has a telephone."

Marlowe got up at once. "You have been getting into communication with Scotland Yard?"

Mr. Gregg shook his head. "No, I haven't. I want to get a bit further off my own bat. You know we have never been able to make much of the Winter's past nor to make out even Mrs. Winter's maiden name, owing to the difficulties of tracing them at Somerset House, Winter being such a common name. There were dozens of John Winters, and we had no guide as to which we wanted, not even the year the marriage took place. Well, the idea came to me yesterday that it might be as well to go over them again. So I sent up Wright, who has the case pretty well at his finger-ends, to see if he could find anything that might be useful to us. I am waiting for his report now." He took up his hat. "Come along, Marlowe."

The ex-constable followed silently. He thought his superior was on the wrong track, but the surprises in the Winter case had been so many that he told himself he was prepared for anything.

Mr. Gregg walked straight across to the post office. Marlowe stood outside the door of the telephone box.

"That you, Wright?" he heard. "Well, what luck?" He could not catch the answer, but the very tone of Mr. Gregg's voice betokened satisfaction, and when he emerged his face was beaming.

He took Marlowe's arm without saying a word, and led him back to his sitting-room, then with the door safely closed he looked at the other with an expression of congratulation.

"We have hit it this time, Marlowe, and no mistake. Wright has found the certificate of marriage by special licence of John Winter and Rosamond Elizabeth Treadstone!"

Chapter Twenty-Four

CARLYN HALL was looking its brightest. Outside, the park was sweet with lilac and syringa, drooping laburnums shone pale gold against a background of evergreens, and everywhere there were May trees in blossom. Inside the house all the preparations for the home-coming of the Squire's bride that had been stopped last year had been set on foot again. Certain rooms that had been got ready for Barbara and closed when the engagement was broken off had been opened again. Everything was putting on its best face for the young mistress who was soon to be brought to it.

Mrs. Carlyn was frankly delighted at the turn things had taken. Yet, as Frank Carlyn got up from the arm-chair and strolled over to the window, his face was gloomy and preoccupied; he looked like anything but a successful lover.

"You will be in at tea-time, Frank?" his mother asked as he stepped out on to the terrace. "The Sheringhams are coming to tennis, and Barbara said she would very likely walk up."

"Oh, yes. I don't know. I expect so," Carlyn rejoined vaguely. "I can't tell, mother. I have promised to go out with Davenant. Ah, there he is."

"Well, really, I can't imagine what Sir Oswald Davenant is about, staying all this time at the 'Carlyn Arms.' And, if he does like this part of the country so much, I wish he would take up his quarters here and behave like a civilized being, instead of sending for you at all sorts of odd times and seasons," Mrs. Carlyn grumbled.

Her son made no answer. He was moving forward to meet Sir Oswald who was coming up to the Hall from the direction of the Home Wood. Like Carlyn he was looking worried and anxious.

"You had my note?" he said, as they got within speaking distance.

"Of course," Carlyn said shortly. "And here I am, though what on earth you want with me I can't make out."

"I told you the time would come when I should claim your help," Sir Oswald went on, ignoring the other's evident ill humour. "You remember what day this is? The anniversary of Winter's death?"

Carlyn nodded. "I am not likely to forget it."

"I hope in future years it may be remembered as the day on which the truth was discovered," Sir Oswald said gravely. "I want you to come with me to the Home Wood, Carlyn."

Carlyn did not make any demur, but there was sullen displeasure in every line of his face, in the hunch of his broad figure, as he walked by Sir Oswald's side.

"Well, I can't get the hang of it all, but you must do as you please," he said at last.

"You will understand it just now I hope and trust," Sir Oswald told him gravely. "For the rest I am much obliged to you for letting me have a free hand, Carlyn."

The other shrugged his shoulders. "Oh, I could do nothing else."

Sir Oswald gave him one keen glance, then he relapsed into silence, a silence that remained unbroken until they had entered the Home Wood and were nearing the gamekeeper's cottage.

Then Sir Oswald stepped behind a clump of rhododendrons, and motioned to Carlyn to follow him. The surprise in the latter's face deepened as he saw that an opening had been carefully arranged through which a view of the front of the cottage could be obtained. In the last day or two a curious change had taken place. All appearance of disuse and decay had been cleared away, it was apparently as trim, the little garden as gay with flowers, as if the Winters had been living there to-day. The door stood half-open and it was evident that some one was moving about inside.

Carlyn turned to Sir Oswald.

"What does it all mean? What is going to happen?"

Sir Oswald hurriedly motioned him to be quiet. "We may not have long to wait!" he whispered. "But you must be absolutely silent."

Carlyn turned aside with an impatient gesture. He had been brought there against his will, and the whole affair seemed to him to be the veriest mummery. He disliked the stirring up of the muddy waters involved in the reopening of the inquiry into Winter's death. Sympathize though he might with Sir Oswald, he had not the faintest belief in Mrs. Winter's innocence; none at all in Sir Oswald's capability of proving it. However, he had no choice but to give the latter the help he claimed, and he resigned himself to the inevitable, and waited, gazing across the clearing at the front of the cottage.

Sir Oswald, for his part, was not looking at the house at all. His eyes were fixed on the undergrowth opposite. When at last he detected a faint movement, he drew a long breath of satisfaction. They had stood there perhaps half an hour, and Carlyn was beginning to feel cramped and restless, when the silence around them, which had been previously uninterrupted, save for the twitter of the birds and the faint multitudinous hum of the insects, was broken by a new sound. There were voices inside the cottage which were raised in anger. It was evident that some altercation was taking place. At last the door was flung violently open—Carlyn stared and rubbed his eyes-—surely the man who strolled rapidly down the path and off in the direction of the Hall bore a curious likeness to himself. His interest was quickened, he leaned forward eagerly.

The perspiration stood on Sir Oswald's brow. His eyes grew very eager as he noted a rustling among the undergrowth.

Another moment and another man came out of the cottage. He was garbed in loose velveteens, and he held a gun which he was examining with some care, but presently with a muttered oath he set it against the garden palings and catching up a spade began to dig in the flower-beds beside.

Carlyn's face grew more and more bewildered. Had it been possible for the dead to revisit their old haunts he would have believed it to be his murdered gamekeeper, John Winter, whom he saw in the flesh before him. He had little time for speculation, however. The bushes Sir Oswald had been watching, were suddenly burst apart. There was an appalling howl—a sound of which Carlyn had never heard the like before, then, quick as a panther, Sir Oswald sprang across and dragged a sobbing, bellowing mass into the open.

"Make a clean breast of it, my lad," he counselled. "It will be best for you in the end."

To his amazement Carlyn saw that the boy was young Jim Retford, his gamekeeper's son. He went across to them.

Retford's sobs redoubled when he saw his master. He tried to tear himself out of Sir Oswald's clasp, to throw himself on the ground. In vain, Sir Oswald's grasp was as firm as a vice.

"Father! Father!" the boy cried. "Don't let him come near me, I never meant no harm." His terrified eyes were fixed upon the figure in the path—a figure that was now standing perfectly still with its back to them. "Don't let him get me!" Softly Retford sobbed.

Sir Oswald set him on his feet and held him there. "He shall not get you if you tell me the truth. If not—" He paused suggestively.

Young Retford howled again. "It wasn't my fault. Dad told me to say naught," he blubbered. "Might have hanged me—they might, and I couldn't know as the gun was loaded."

"What?" a curious change came over Sir Oswald's face, but his hold on the boy did not relax. "What was it you never meant to do?" he demanded sternly, giving him a shake. "Speak the truth, lad."

Young Retford's teeth chattered, his legs tottered under him. "I never meant to harm John Winter," he howled, amid a fresh paroxysm of sobbing. "I had just come up here to see if I could find our Esther, what was lost and the gun stood by the gate. I took it up and it went off in my hand and shot him right in the face. Oh, oh, oh!"

Sir Oswald drew a deep breath. "So that is the solution of the Home Wood mystery. To think it never occurred to any of us before. Why did you not speak out and tell the truth, Jim Retford?"

"Father told me not, sir," the boy sobbed. "Many a man has been hanged for less, he said, or shut up in a reformatory. And that would have killed me, too, sir. So I never said a word, not till he came back to make me," with a shuddering glance at the cottage garden from which the figure had disappeared now.

Carlyn took off his hat and passed his hand over his forehead, staring at the boy in amazement. "So you mean to tell us that it—was you who killed John Winter," he said slowly.

"I never meant to do it, sir." The lad's grimy, tear-stained face was contorted anew. "And Father—Father said—oh, oh!" And he made a last desperate attempt to free himself.

Carlyn saw that his keeper was hurrying towards them from a side path. His face was white and frightened.

"Let the lad go, sir," he said heavily. "I will make a clean breast of it."

Carlyn turned to him almost savagely.

"Do you mean to say that you have known all the time that your son killed Winter, and you have allowed an innocent woman to be hunted all over the country for it?" he demanded sternly.

"'Twasn't my fault that Mrs. Winter ran away," Retford said sullenly. "That was what made folks say it was her. If she had bided at home there would have been no harm done."

"At any rate you have done harm enough—you and your son," Carlyn thundered. His share of the family temper was beginning to assert itself. Sir Oswald touched his arm, others were coming on the scene. Garth Davenant and a stranger were emerging from the cottage, the Inspector of Police and one of his subordinates were following Retford up the path. Sir Oswald addressed himself to these two latter. "I promised you, you should find your work done for you, didn't I, inspector? Now I charge this boy, James Retford, on his own confession, with having caused the death of John Winter, and his father, Robert Retford, with being an accessory after the fact."

"I shall have to get a warrant, sir," the man was beginning when Retford interrupted him.

"You needn't bother yourself, inspector. We will go quietly with you, I promise you. For me, I shall be glad enough to get the thing off my chest. It was a big mistake when I didn't tell all about it at the time. It was two years ago to-day, sir." Insensibly he looked away from the others, and addressed himself to Carlyn.

"We were in sore trouble at home and I was in a rare way about it. I was on my way back to work after I had had my bit of dinner when, coming along, I heard a shot. I thought nothing of it at the moment, but I had only gone a few steps further when I met my boy Jim. He was nearly mad with fright, but I made him tell me what he had done, how he had taken up Winter's gun and pointed it at him, not dreaming it was loaded, and how it had gone off in his hands and killed the keeper. I didn't suppose the man was really dead, I thought the gun had gone off and hurt him a bit, but when I got to the cottage I saw the lad was right enough, Winter was dead, and a ghastly sight at that."

"But why on earth didn't you tell people that it was an accident? Why didn't you go for help?" Carlyn questioned excitedly.

Retford scratched his head in a puzzled fashion.

"It seemed to me as we might not have been believed. I was a fool. I see that plain enough now. But I had lost one child, or as good as lost her, and I thought I couldn't run the risk of losing the other. Jim there, he wasn't the poor creature then that he is now—but a fine upstanding lad he was, just the pride of my life. It came across me that they might think he had done it on purpose, or they might have said he wasn't under proper control, and sent him away from us to a reformatory or something of that kind. I lost my head, sir, that is what it come to, and when my senses did come back to me it was too late to speak out, least it seemed so to me. But I always thought as they would have said it was an accident; I never guessed they would think it was murder, and if Mrs. Winter had been took I should have spoke out. That is all, sir."

His head sank on his breast as he finished, his son was leaning against a tree trunk close at hand, the picture of abject misery.

The inspector, after conferring for a minute with Sir Oswald and Carlyn beckoned to them.

"You had better come down to the station with me, Mr. Retford, you and your boy, and we will have all this put down in writing."

The keeper made no demur. He turned quietly with the policeman, Jim shambling along in his wake.

Frank Carlyn stared after them in a state bordering on stupefaction.

Sir Oswald touched his arm. "Come, we must follow them, our evidence may be wanted."

Carlyn turned and stared at him, "What in Heaven's name made you suspect this?"

Sir Oswald shook his head. "As a matter of fact I did not suspect this. I felt sure that Retford knew something of the matter. An accident showed me that young Retford was in the habit of coming here most days. Instinct told me he would be here to-day, and with Garth's help I arranged that little tableau, hoping to frighten the truth out of him. Garth and his friends are capital amateur actors, and I got the idea of reconstructing the crime partly from the French Police and partly from 'The Bells.' You remember Irving's big scene? But I must confess I really suspected his father, who I fancied had shot Winter in his rage at his daughter's betrayal. However, it seems I was wrong, and the Home Wood mystery turns out to have been accidental, and no murder at all."

Carlyn held out his hand.

"I can't realize it yet. But I congratulate you most heartily, Davenant, and later on I shall hope to have an opportunity of congratulating Lady Davenant personally."

Chapter Twenty-Five

ROSAMOND TREADSTONE tapped at the door of her stepmother's room. It was very early, none of the household were astir yet, but the door was thrown open instantly, and Lady Treadstone herself appeared fully dressed.

"I was expecting you," she said in a dull, level tone, "come in." She closed the door behind them and stood and looked at the girl. She herself was very pale, and her eyes were dim and weary, her hair had grown visibly greyer in the past few weeks.

Rosamond drew her to the open window. Her hands as she laid them on Lady Treadstone's arm felt hot and feverish, two red spots burned on her cheeks, her grey eyes had dark shadows under them, the pupils were dilated.

"Look here," she said impatiently.

She pointed to the water washing the foot of the rock gleaming in the sunrise. Porthcawel lay behind. They had a glimpse of the open sea as they gazed westwards. But it was not on the blue, rippling water that Lady Treadstone's eyes were fixed in a kind of horrified fascination, but on a tiny boat that lay on the water a little way out. At first sight there was nothing alarming about it. It held two men who were doing nothing but lie back in their seats, letting the placid sea drift it where it would.

"I saw them directly I opened my eyes," Lady Treadstone said beneath her breath. "Rosamond, what does it mean?"

"The end," the girl said quietly, "it is no use fighting against it any longer, mother. I have known it was inevitable since I met

Marlowe on the beach, but I wish for your sake it had happened at the Priory, that I had never come here. I only bring trouble on everyone." She burst into choking sobs.

Lady Treadstone drew her gently to a chair. "Hush, child!" she said, her own voice trembling. "Never say that. Now we must not give way. We must think what we can do—how we can save you, get you away."

Rosamond shook her head.

"It is too late. We are watched on all sides. No, this time Marlowe has won and I have lost. I don't know that it would matter much"—with a dreary sob—"that it would not be for the best, for I am tired of a life of lies and subterfuge, but for the trouble it must bring on you, the disgrace to my father's name."

Lady Treadstone laid her hand on the down-bent, golden head.

"We must face it bravely if it comes—for your dear father's sake," she whispered.

Rosamond sat still for a minute. Lady Treadstone waited, her hands still mutely caressing the pretty, ruffled hair, her eyes still watching the boat with the two silent men. At last the younger woman spoke in a harsh, unnatural voice.

"I don't know. It is wisest sometimes to run away. And when I can't stand the thought of it all, when it comes to me in the night, and I realize the shame, the publicity, it comforts me to remember that there are still ways left, that one plunge into the deep water there"—she threw her hands outward—"would end it all, would set us free."

Lady Treadstone shivered.

"Ah, no, no, Rose," she said, recurring to the old childish name, "your father's daughter would never choose the coward's way. It will soon be over, Rose. We will engage the cleverest lawyers in England, and you will be free. And then—there will be Oswald to think of."

"Yes, there will be Oswald to think of," Rosamond repeated. She sprang to her feet shaking off her stepmother's gentle, detaining hand, and leaning against the window frame, a tragic figure with her white strained face, the droop of her strong, young figure. In some indescribable way she seemed to have shrunk in the last few days. Her gown hung loosely upon her, the masses of golden hair seemed to overshadow the small, peaked face. "There will be Oswald to think of," she said once more, "there is Oswald to think of"—her voice gaining in strength—"when I remember him, mother, his love and goodness to me, then it—the water—seems the only possible end. Haven't you realized that he is a very proud man, and I"—with a pitiful gesture of self-abandonment—"am not a wife to be proud of, am I? Yes, there will always be Oswald to think of. Merciful Heaven, if I could only forget."

Lady Treadstone made no answer, save that her lips moved slightly, but no sound came. Out there on the water there were three boats. One stood out some little distance, the other two were moving nearer. The two men who had been motionless so long were bending to their oars; they were making for the rock. The very sight seemed to paralyse Lady Treadstone; she was absolutely incapable of movement; her very brain was benumbed. Vaguely she felt that there were things that ought to be done, that Rosamond ought to be saved in spite of herself, yet she could do nothing but stand there and watch and wait. From the boats her eyes wandered to a large portrait of her husband, painted by a well-known Academician, that hung over the fireplace. It was a wonderful likeness; one could have fancied he had just been speaking; the smile still lingered in the keen, grey eyes, round the firm, well-cut mouth. She shivered as she asked herself what he would have said, what he would have done if he had known of the fate awaiting his dearly loved, only child. That

he had died literally of a broken heart at his daughter's deser-
tion of him and the manner of it, his widow knew only too well.
Though she had been his first love, though his heart had been
faithful to her through all the circumstances of their parting,
Lady Treadstone had felt herself powerless to comfort him, as
she felt powerless now to help Rosamond herself.

As the two stood there waiting, there was a knock at the big
front door of the Hold, a ring that echoed through the whole
house. Rosamond turned slowly and faced the door. In her
beautiful eyes was the look of some wild creature brought suddenly to bay. Another moment, and the expected summons
came, Greyson white and trembling, opened the door.

"Missie, Missie, my dear, there are two men asking for you
in the hall, but don't you go, my dearie, it is only over our dead
bodies that they shall get you."

"Dear old nursie." The girl came swiftly across the room. In
a measure some of her old strength and vitality was restored to
her, some of the old imperious ring to her voice. She stooped
and kissed the old woman's wrinkled cheeks. "It's no use, nursie
dear, I must speak to them. You wait here with her ladyship."
She moved to the door.

But her words aroused Lady Treadstone from the terrified apathy that seemed to have come over her. She followed
her quickly.

"I am going with you Rosamond. Dear, you did not think I
should let you go alone."

A pathetic smile curved Rosamond's lips. "Very soon I shall
have to be alone. But for now—if you will come."

She went on, walking erectly, with firm, regular steps.
Lady Treadstone and Greyson followed, their faces white and
frightened. Lady Treadstone rested her hand for a minute
within the maid's.

Two men were standing in the hall, Inspector Church and Marlowe. The light of victory was in the latter's eyes. At last he had won! The chase had been long and difficult, more than once he had been checkmated, but at last the game was his. He felt no pity for the woman coming down the stairs; to him she was the prey who had escaped him so long, nothing more.

Rosamond's step did not hesitate or falter, she came straight across the hall to them. "You wish to speak to me, I think?" she said in her clear tones, that now sounded cold, indifferent even.

"We did, madam," Inspector Church said awkwardly. He felt momentarily abashed. This queenly-looking woman with the weary eyes, the crown of golden hair, was so unlike his pre-conceived notions of the gamekeeper's wife for whom they had been looking so long that for the time he felt overwhelmed. He pulled himself together, however, and pulled an official looking paper from his pocket. "I am sorry to say that I am here in the execution of my duty, madam. Rosamond Elizabeth Winter, otherwise Treadstone, I arrest you for the wilful murder of your husband, John Winter, at Carlyn, on May 6th, 19—. And it is my duty to warn you that anything you say in answer to the charge will be taken down in writing, and may be used against you," he hurried over the words rather, keeping his eyes fixed on the girl's face.

But Rosamond gave no sign of shrinking or of fear. "I understand," she said quietly. "And you want me to come with you now. Well, I am ready." She moved a step nearer the door, while the two men stared at her.

But Lady Treadstone hurried after her. "Child, child, what are you doing? You can't go like this. And where you go I go, remember that."

Rosamond's face softened momentarily. She touched the elder woman's hand gently. "No, no, dear, you can't come with me. Stay here, mother, and some day perhaps I may come back to you."

"Your father would have gone with you and I am going," Lady Treadstone repeated firmly, but the tears were trembling in her eyes, she was shaking from head to foot in her agitation.

Inspector Church stepped forward.

"You can't go with the prisoner, my lady. Of course, if you care to follow you will be able to see her after the charge has been read. In the meantime, my good woman, can't you get your mistress's coat and hat?" He addressed himself to Greyson, who was weeping and praying audibly.

Already some knowledge of what was going on has permeated to the servants of the Hold. They were gathering in groups, at the other end of the hall, there was a sound of sobs, and muttered threats from the men. Inspector Church was anxious to get away. As soon as Rosamond's things had been brought he motioned to her that they were ready to start.

Rosamond glanced round lingeringly as they made their way to the private landing-stage. Was she seeing it all for the last time, she wondered, the peace and beauty of the Rock and the Hold? Was it possible that she was exchanging her ordered life there for the dreary solitude of a prison cell, it might even be for death itself? Her breath caught in a sob as she asked herself the question. Involuntarily she put up her hands to her throat. But the sense of unreality, of which she had been conscious ever since she had seen that the arrest was inevitable clung to her still. She felt as though she was taking part in some pageant or play; she could not realize that she, Rosamond Treadstone, was really in this terrible danger.

On the landing-stage there were more policemen, several boats were moored alongside, another was coming swiftly across the shining water from Porthcawel. But all the attention of Inspector Church and his men was given to their prisoner. Not until the boat had come in alongside, and the three men in her were springing out did they realize that a new element had entered into the situation. Sir Oswald Davenant was the first to land. His whole aspect had altered. A weight of care had rolled off his shoulders and he seemed years younger; his expression was glad and triumphant. Frank Carlyn, and a third man, who bore upon him plainly the stamp of officialdom, followed.

A red flush streaked the prisoner's white cheeks as she recognized them. Sir Oswald glanced from her to Inspector Church.

"Stop!" he cried in his clear ringing tones. "Inspector, you have made a few mistakes over this miserable business; now you are just about to make another. You—"

"I don't think so," the inspector interrupted him. "I am sorry you are here, Sir Oswald Davenant, but I think you will understand that there can be no interference with the course of my duty."

Sir Oswald laughed as he glanced from him to Marlowe.

"In a short time you will probably be very glad that I came; yes, Mr. Marlowe, once more you have had all your trouble for nothing. While you have been following a false scent I hold in my pocket the confession of the real criminal. Mr. Carlyn and Superintendent Quin from Carlyn can confirm my statement."

"Impossible!" The inspector was beginning when with a quick exclamation Sir Oswald sprang past him.

The reaction had been too much for Rosamond. The long strain of the past years culminating in this morning's horror had beaten down even her splendid vitality. As she heard her lover's words it seemed to her that everything was whirling round her, the glittering sun, the policemen, even Sir Oswald himself. With a low cry she staggered forward and fell unconscious to the ground just as Sir Oswald reached her.

Chapter Twenty-Six

"And the prince married the Princess with the raven locks, and they lived happy ever afterwards?" Maisie questioned, in her clear, childish treble.

"Yes, I suppose they did," Rosamond assented with a slow smile.

Maisie clasped her hands. "Oh, you do tell nice stories. Almost as nice as my dear Miss Martin used to."

Rosamond raised her eyebrows. "Almost, not quite."

Maisie considered the point for a moment with her head on one side. "Not quite, I think," she decided at last, loyal to her first friend. "Though yours are very nice too, Miss Treadstone," she added politely.

"And why are mine not quite as nice?" Rosamond asked teasingly.

Maisie thought a minute. "I think perhaps it is the voice," she announced at last. "Though you often make me think of her, Miss Treadstone. But Miss Martin had a nice, strong voice, and yours is very weak, so that I have to listen very intently."

"And don't you like listening intently?" Rosamond laughed. "Perhaps my voice is weak because I am weak myself, Maisie."

She certainly looked weak enough for anything as she spoke. She was half-sitting, half-lying in a nest of cushions on the settee in Lady Treadstone's morning-room at the Hold. She was very thin, her once rounded figure was wasted almost to attenuation, her short hair was curling in red gold tendrils all over her head; her face was absolutely colourless, save for the blue half-circles underneath her eyes, but it wore a look of peace and rest such as Elizabeth Martin had never known.

Spring had merged into summer, summer had become autumn, and was rapidly approaching winter, and still

Rosamond Treadstone lay ill and prostrate at the Hold. For weeks after she had learned the truth about John Winter's death she had lain between life and death, and only very slowly had it become apparent that the former was to conquer. But now it seemed as though, having reached a certain point, she had no strength to go farther. Her days were passed in a sort of mental apathy, and her prostration had been so prolonged that the doctors were becoming seriously anxious. Nothing seemed to have the power to rouse her, and it had been Sir Oswald who had suggested sending for Maisie in the hope that the child she loved might have power to interest Rosamond. His plan had proved more successful than he had dared to hope. Rosamond had been unmistakably pleased to see the child, and Maisie charmed with the resemblance she detected to her dear Miss Martin had taken to her at once. Much of her time was spent with Rosamond in the morning-room, and the doctors had been delighted when they learned that her demand for stories had been acceded to. To-day, they were talking of moving their patient to a warmer climate as soon as her strength was a little more maintained. Sir Oswald had his own ideas as to how this was to be effected, but he had said nothing to Rosamond yet.

Though there had naturally been all sorts of rumours, Rosamond Treadstone's name had been successfully kept out of the papers when the Home Wood mystery had been finally cleared up, and her marriage with Winter had not been made public. Where once his death had been shown to have been the result of an accident, there had been little interest taken in the affair, and already it was becoming forgotten. But this, Rosamond, obsessed as she had been by the thought of the death, could not realize, and she had a morbid fear of being recognized. Only with Maisie did she feel quite safe, and the child's affection and trust were very soothing.

She smiled now as Maisie nestled up to her with a demand for another story, and laid her hand on the child's curls lovingly. Just then Lady Treadstone came into the room.

"I want you to read this, Rosamond," she said, handing her a letter. "Maisie, your father is asking for you. He has been into Porthcawel, and I think he has some sweets for a good little girl."

The child ran away and Lady Treadstone turned back to her stepdaughter.

"You see. Barbara wants to pay you a visit. Frank and she will be quite near. You will let them come, won't you, Rosamond?"

"Oh, I don't think so." The girl shivered among her cushions. "Barbara was very good to me, but it would bring all that dreadful time back."

"I am sorry, dear," Lady Treadstone said regretfully. "I think it would do you good to see a fresh face, but—" She turned aside and began to arrange some flowers she had brought in.

Rosamond's lips quivered.

"She was very kind to me but it was for Frank's sake and because she is an angel of pity. She thought me guilty, every one did. Even you sometimes, mother—" with a quick glance.

"Oh, Rosamond!" Lady Treadstone dropped her flowers, her eyes filled with tears.

"Didn't you?" Rosamond asked quietly.

"Never! Never!" Lady Treadstone said passionately. "I always said to myself that your father's little Rose must be innocent. If I have doubted you once or twice, oh, forgive me, child, it has only been a passing thought."

"I knew it," Rosamond said softly. She drew her stepmother's face down to hers, and kissed it gently. "You have been so good to me mother. And how could you help doubting? Why sometimes"—with a terrified look round—"when I have wakened in the night in the dark, I have even doubted myself. All sorts of fears and fancies have crowded into my brain."

"Ah, well! It is all over now," said Lady Treadstone, stroking the girl's hair. "And you do forgive me, Rosamond?"

Rosamond turned her lips to the soft hand. "Forgive you my more than mother! I shall be grateful for your kindness all the days of my life."

Lady Treadstone was about to make some rejoinder when Sir Oswald's step was heard in the passage and she turned to meet him.

"Wish me good luck, dear Lady Treadstone," he said as she smiled at him.

"The best of luck," she said, pressing his hand.

He went straight across to Rosamond. "How are you to-day, sweetheart?"

A faint pink flushed the white cheeks at the tender word.

"A little better, I think," she answered uncertainly. "At least, I don't know, I think Maisie does me good."

"Dr. Spencer says you are better, much better," Sir Oswald said, taking the chair behind her. "I have just been talking to him and he says that, now you are well enough to travel, we should lose no time in getting you away. I want you to come with me." His tone was quite matter of fact, Rosamond looked at him half uncomprehendingly. "I want you to come with me," he repeated. "Dear, I have been very patient, but now I want a wife."

Rosamond's colour deepened, but her grey eyes met his unfalteringly.

"Impossible! I shall never marry. Can't you see that?"

"No, I can't," said Sir Oswald sturdily. "In the Sunny South you will soon get well and strong."

"It isn't only a question of health," Rosamond said quickly, "though no man wants an invalid wife, but—"

"I want this invalid," he interrupted her fondly.

"But there is everything else," she went on as if she had not heard him. "How would you like it to be known—how would you like Maisie to know—that you had married John Winter's widow?"

Sir Oswald leaned forward.

"I should not mind one atom," he said easily. "You silly child, so that is the phantom that has stood between us, that has been worrying you all this time, as for what the world knows or guesses, it does not matter that"—snapping his fingers—"and people don't trouble about it as much as you think. They haven't time to bother about such things nowadays. As for Maisie, if she knew her dear Miss Martin's identical with that of the wonderful new mother she is going to have, she would be overjoyed. As for myself—" he paused, and looked at her steadily. "For your sake, dearest, I wish you had not made a mistake in the past. I hate to think you were once Winter's wife, as I should hate to think you ever belonged to any man but me, but I would not on that account forgo one moment of the golden future we are to spend together. I grudge every little bit of it that you pass away from me."

Rosamond pushed her curls back from her brow wearily.

"I wish I knew what I ought to do. But I am so tired I don't seem able even to think. But something tells me it isn't right."

Sir Oswald took both the thin, hot hands in his and held them in his strong, firm clasp.

"And I tell you it is right, most divinely right," he said, in his clear, decided tones. "You must let me do the thinking for you. You must forget the past, it is over and done with. The present is ours, and the future, the happy future that we are going to spend together. And you must not keep me waiting long. I want to take you away before the real winter begins. Can you be ready in a week?"

"A week!" Rosamond lay still and looked at him. "You must be dreaming. It is impossible!"

"I don't think so," he prisoned both her hands in one of his, and passed his other arm round her amid the cushions. "I am going to settle things my own way," he added masterfully. "You have been an autocrat long enough. We will be married on Monday week, and my yacht will be waiting to take us to Madeira. What do you say to that?"

Rosamond glanced at him as she met the look in his eyes, hers veiled themselves in their long lashes.

"It doesn't seem much use my saying anything," she said, a tiny smile stealing round her mouth, "since you have made up your mind."

Sir Oswald and Lady Davenant have been married some years now, and Rosamond's identity with John Winter's widow has never been discovered. In the peerage the entry runs: "Rosamond Elizabeth only daughter of the seventh Lord Tread-stone, born May 1st, 18—; married 19— to Sir Oswald Davenant, Bart., of Davenant Priory." And so the history of that first terrible mistake of hers has never leaked out.

The change in her hair and appearance was so great when she went back to the Priory as its mistress that even the Dowager Lady Davenant never discovered that she was the pseudo-governess. Sir Oswald had taken care that almost all the servants were new; only two of the old ones were left, the butler and Latimer, and if those two have ever suspected anything—and sometimes a hazy doubt that they may have done so has crossed Rosamond Davenant's mind—they have never breathed a word of it.

Sir Oswald and his wife pass most of their time at the Priory, for that time of stress and trial through which they have passed has left its mark to some extent on both of them. Sir Oswald's eyes, though sufficiently serviceable, will never be quite what they were before his accident, and Rosamond, though her splendid health and vitality have reasserted themselves in a greater degree than the doctors at one time dared to hope, is to some extent a sufferer from nerves, and is happiest in the country with her husband and their children.

For there are other children at the Priory now; though Maisie remains the only daughter, there are three big, bonny boys in the nursery—three boys who have their mother's lovely colouring and their father's strength and length of limb, and who are the pride of their father's heart. Rosamond is rather glad they are all boys; she does not want any other girl to take Maisie's place, and Maisie, for her part, is devoted to her beautiful stepmother and her little brothers. Quite the fastest friends of the Davenants are the Carlyns. Every year the latter come to the Priory for a long visit. The Davenant boys are devoted to Barbara's little girl, and sometimes, Rosamond, looking into the distant future, fancies she sees a vision of what one daughter-in-law will be like.

Sybil Lorrimer is dead. She married an officer and was killed in a carriage accident a year later. Her coadjutor, Marlowe, is still with Gregg and Stubbs, but he has not risen in his profession as he hoped to do.

THE END

Lightning Source UK Ltd.
Milton Keynes UK
UKOW06f0413260216

269156UK00001B/36/P